In the still darkness of the car, Keir's voice throbbed strangely. The hand that had restrained her took her chin in a firm but gentle grip, turning her head towards him.

'Wait,' he said huskily. 'I don't believe I told you how very lovely you look tonight.' The words were a simple enough compliment, one she had received many times before. But she had never been so strongly affected.

There was a moment of intensity before he said her name fiercely. Then he was kissing her with a stinging passion and his hands were inside her coat, moving the length of her body.

As they continued their exploration she was beyond protesting; she ought to deny the intimacies his hands were seeking, but she couldn't. Suddenly, he reached up and flicked on the interior light.

'Was it like that with my brother Tris, Venna?' he demanded harshly. 'I have to know.'

She looked wonderingly at him, so that there was no need for him to say as he did, harshly, 'Look at me, Venna! Take a good, long look, so that you'll know me again. Because I'm going to make damned sure that you never forget what *I* look like!'

A QUESTION OF LOVE

BY

ANNABEL MURRAY

MILLS & BOON LIMITED
ETON HOUSE   18-24 PARADISE ROAD
RICHMOND   SURREY   TW9 1SR

First published in Great Britain 1988 by Mills & Boon Limited

© Annabel Murray 1988

Australian copyright 1988 Philippine copyright 1988 This edition 1988

ISBN 0 263 76138 X

Set in Times Roman 10 on 11 pt. 01-8811-58583 C

Made and printed in Great Britain

For Tom
and all his golfing friends

CHAPTER ONE

'Hello, Gemma darling.' Venna Leigh swept the blonde toddler up into her arms and hugged her. In return she received a moist, somewhat sticky, kiss. 'Has she been good today, Carol?' she asked the friend who acted as child-minder for her.

'She's been as good as gold,' the older woman assured her. 'But isn't she always? Sometimes I think your Gemma's too good to be true.'

'Don't say that!' Venna shivered. 'It makes me superstitious. It sounds like "too good to live". I don't know *what* I'd do if I lost Gemma.'

'You worry about her too much,' Carol Wood assured her, but her expression was sympathetic as she looked at the small red-headed girl who looked too slight and delicate to bear the weight of her self-imposed responsibilities. It was hard to believe that this diminutive, lovely creature also had a first-class brain and that Venna had gained a good degree in English Literature at Cambridge. Despite her looks and bubbly personality, Venna, Carol knew, was a serious-minded, extremely hard-working young woman. But she had looked more than usually tired lately, Carol thought. Working full-time and coping with a toddler in the evenings was no joke. Especially when Venna received no support from the one person from whom she was entitled to expect it, her fiancé. But even fatigue couldn't detract from the girl's unusual beauty, Carol decided, or dim the sparkle in those enormous, startlingly green eyes. 'You know Gemma's as fit as a fiddle,' she went on bracingly, then, 'Got time for a cuppa?'

'Oh, I'd love one!' Venna said with feeling. 'It's foul out. It's been sleeting all day.' She ran a hand through the polished mahogany of her hair, demonstrating that it was still damp after her dash from her car to the front door of Carol's Birkdale home. 'Next thing we know it'll be snow! And the shop's been like a madhouse.' But it wasn't really a complaint. Venna loved her work and dealt competently with its demands. She was half-owner of Classics, a Southport shop which dealt in both new and antiquarian books. Even now in mid-winter they were still doing a fairly steady trade, much to Venna's relief, for most of her capital was tied up in the partnership.

Still cradling the child, she followed her friend into the living-room, where half a dozen other small children looked up briefly from their absorbed play. 'I don't know how you manage it,' Venna congratulated her friend. 'It takes me nearly all my spare time and energy to keep one child amused.'

'Experience!' The older woman laughed. 'Don't forget I've had four of my own. Mind you, half an hour ago things were very different. There was a free-for-all over who was going to ride the rocking-horse. Because she was the only non-contestant, I let Gemma have it.'

Venna put Gemma down and sank on to a comfortable, if somewhat child-worn, sofa. She looked round her appreciatively and absorbed, as she always did, the welcoming, homely atmosphere of Carol's house. Though the room was shabby, it was filled with evidences of domestic life—the many family photographs, Jim Wood's favourite pipe left on a corner of the mantelpiece. It made her neat, functional flat seem even lonelier by comparison.

'I must say I'm ready for this myself.' Carol emerged from the kitchen carrying a tray. 'So what went wrong at the shop today?' she asked, but Venna was momentarily diverted from her woes.

'Home-made cake!' she exclaimed. 'And I bet you've made it today in the midst of all this.' She gestured to the toddlers whom Carol Wood minded on a regular basis for several working mothers besides herself. 'I do envy you. I enjoy running a business and I wouldn't want to give it up altogether, but sometimes I just crave domesticity for a change.' Then, in answer to the other woman's query, 'The shop? Oh, just about everything went wrong that could. You get days like that. Nothing I couldn't deal with, of course.'

'You had plenty of customers by the sound of things.' Carol poured the tea. 'That's the important thing, isn't it?'

'Oh, yes, but today they were either just looking or wanted things we hadn't got. One man was quite rude because he'd been waiting a month for a book. I explained politely that it can take a long time to track down an out-of-print edition. But he went on as if it were just a matter of picking up the phone and bingo!'

'And how was that fiancé of yours today?' Carol asked, motioning to Venna to take one of the generous slices of cake. 'Go on,' she urged. 'You *won't* get fat. You're too thin by half. You work too hard.'

'Terry was at a sale all morning. There were some books he particularly wanted. Some out-of-town dealer bumped the prices up to ridiculous levels. But like an idiot, Terry went on bidding. He does annoy me sometimes. He paid far more than we'd agreed, and that led to us having an argument and finally a row about everything in general.' For a moment the corners of Venna's generous mouth drooped, but a happy gurgle from baby Gemma, who was now playing happily with a set of building-blocks, brought an answering smile to her face. 'Don't mind me,' she told her friend more cheerfully. 'I'll get over it. I always do.'

'I suppose the usual subject cropped up?' Carol inclined her head towards the child. As Venna nodded,

Carol went on, 'He's jealous of her, of course. It would be different if she were his own.'

'Perhaps.' Venna's large green eyes were troubled. 'Sometimes I think Terry doesn't really like children. The only thing he seems to be passionate about is books. I can understand that, of course. They fascinate me too. But you have to keep a sense of proportion. We're business people, not rich collectors.'

'Has he said any more about getting married?'

'He brings it up about once a week. Once or twice lately I've nearly said yes. But somehow something keeps holding me back from that final commitment. I'm lonely, Carol.' It was said without self-pity, but the older woman recognised the poignancy that lay beneath the words. 'I want to get married, and though I wouldn't be without Gemma, I want to have a family of my own.'

'And so you should,' Carol said warmly. 'You'd make an excellent mother—and wife,' she added with deliberate emphasis. She hesitated, then, half apologetically, 'I know she was your sister—half-sister, I should say— and I don't like to speak ill of the dead. But I do think Shelagh was totally irresponsible, doing what she did. Why on earth did she want a baby so desperately? I only met her a couple of times, but she didn't strike me as being the maternal sort.'

'She might have given you that impression, but she'd always been mad about babies for as long as I can remember.' Venna smiled a little sadly at the memory. 'When we were small, her favourite game was playing at mummies. She had a huge collection of baby dolls— her family, she called them. She used to let me help her bathe and dress them.'

'Babies are rather different from dolls,' Carol said wryly.

'True. But as we grew up she was always talking about the real babies we'd have one day. She was always looking in prams. She'd even chosen names for her children. She used to treat me as her baby too. I don't remember it myself, but apparently she was the one who encouraged me to walk. And then when we went to school she always used to stand up for me. I was tiny as a child, and some of the bigger children would have bullied me if Shelagh had let them.'

'And in all these plans of hers, was a husband never taken into account?' Carol asked curiously.

'At that age, I don't think it crossed our minds that a husband had anything to do with babies. Neither of us could really remember our fathers. Shelagh's Dad left Mum when Shelagh was only two, and I was about the same age when my father went off. You know Mum died of cancer when we were still quite young? Shelagh was only thirteen. I was eleven. So then we came up north, to Preston, to live with Granny Birtles, and she was always going on about women being better off without men.'

Their mother's story, the desertion of two husbands, repeated over and over again by their grandmother, a kind but strait-laced disciplinarian with a strong moral code, had affected the two girls in different ways. Shelagh, the elder of the two, was all for a life independent of what she called the male con-trick of marriage. Venna, a romantic at heart despite her grandmother's dictums, longed for love, marriage and security.

'I still think Shelagh was selfish,' Carol persisted, and though Venna wished she wouldn't talk that way she knew Carol's indignation was on her behalf. 'She was a bit short-sighted, too,' her friend added, 'considering she was a solicitor. She hadn't even made a will, had she?'

'No, but then, I don't suppose she'd expected to die so young.' Venna sighed. 'Poor Shelagh. I still miss her. We were good friends, which isn't always the case with half-sisters. And honestly, Carol, if you'd known her better you'd realise she hadn't a selfish bone in her body. In fact, it was her thoughtfulness for others that led to her accident.'

'How was that? I thought she was in a car crash.'

'She was. She'd driven out of London, down into Kent, to visit a client. This woman was an invalid, and though it was just about possible for her to get to Shelagh's office, Shelagh wouldn't hear of it. It was on the way back that she was in the pile-up. She was killed outright. It was terrible.' Remembering, Venna bit her lip and her voice quivered a little as she went on, 'Gemma was in the nursery as usual that day, and I was away on holiday. Shelagh's landlady looked after Gemma until she could contact me. You can imagine the shock I had.'

'I can! Poor Venna, it must have been awful, and you were only twenty-four when she died. Wasn't there anyone else to look after Gemma?'

'No. Granny Birtles was dead, of course. It was our legacies from her that enabled me to go into business with Terry and meant Shelagh could afford to have a child and pay nursery fees and so on. Granny Birtles was quite well-to-do, you see. Grandad Birtles had been something big in the textile world. He died long before we went to live with Granny, but she'd invested all his money and done very well out of it.

'Poor Granny. She'd have been heartbroken, not just because she loved Shelagh, which she did, of course, but because Shelagh had done something so totally against everything Granny believed in.'

'You've mentioned some aunts who still live in Preston. What about them? Couldn't they have helped?'

Venna chuckled.

'Nora, Dora and Aurora. They're great-aunts actually, Granny Birtles' sisters—her name was Laura! I think my great-grandparents must have been a bit dotty. When I was a kid I used to get the aunts all mixed up.

Their names seemed to be interchangeable. You know, like masks in a comic farce.'

'They'd be too elderly to cope with a small child.'

'Lord, yes. Anyway, Nora and Dora were shocked to the core. They struck Shelagh out of the family bible. That was the ultimate in disapproval. Aurora was sympathetic. Up till then she'd always been the black sheep of the family—an illicit love affair with a married man, and a vicar to boot! But I wouldn't trust Aurora to look after a baby. She's far too vague and eccentric.'

'Did—what were their names?—Nora and Dora disapprove of you too, because you stuck by Shelagh?'

'Yes, but more in sorrow than in anger. They still allow me to go and visit them. I'm glad. I'm very fond of the aunts. I was always closer to them than Shelagh was. Especially Dora. It was her husband Lionel who taught me to love books and told me everything I know about the book trade.'

'I think you've mentioned him before. Isn't he an antiquarian book dealer himself?'

'Yes. He's got a quaint little back-street shop in Preston, crammed to overflowing with books and ephemera. Actually, I think he rather dreads anyone buying anything. He hates to part with a single volume. He and Dora never had any children and I think the books took their place with him. I used to help him in the school holidays.'

'I suppose that's what made you decide to go into the book trade.'

'Not at first. But when I came down from university I still hadn't decided what I was going to do. There weren't many jobs going, anyway. So he asked me if I'd like to work for him and learn the trade. I stayed with him two years. Then Granny Birtles died and left me all that money, and my great-uncle Lionel advised me to branch out on my own. We watched the advertisements in the trade magazines and saw Terry's advert for a partner, here in Southport. I applied, got it, and bingo, here I am.'

'And you enjoy it, don't you? But it's hard work being in the shop all day and looking after a small child at night. If only Shelagh had told you who the father of her child was.'

'I'm glad she didn't,' Venna said quickly. 'I've loved looking after Gemma. And anyway, I wouldn't have contacted the father. He might have taken Gemma away. I didn't approve of what Shelagh did either, but it's not the child's fault. And everything would be all right if only Terry would agree to adopt her.' She shrugged slender shoulders. 'I'm very fond of Terry, you know. He's not a bad sort. It's just that he can be very pig-headed about some things. The real trouble is that we're both quick-tempered.' She sighed. 'I try so hard not to be, but every so often I just break out. Gran always used to say it was this red hair of mine.'

'I don't know Terry, of course,' Carol said. 'Except from seeing him in the shop. But from what you've told me at various times he doesn't sound to me like the man for you.' Privately Carol thought Terry Little was irritatingly juvenile, with his tight velvet trousers, fancy shirts and blond hair swept back into a pony-tail. At twenty-six, it was about time he grew out of such affectations. But Venna was well aware of her friend's opinion.

'Goodness, do I really go on about him that much? It makes me sound very disloyal, and I don't mean to be. I know you find him a bit unconventional, Carol, the way he dresses and everything. But he says the image suits our business, and certainly he's popular with the customers. My main concern is that I've got to be absolutely certain I'm doing the right thing,' Venna went on almost to herself. And it was an inner dialogue in which she had indulged more and more just recently.

'Not just for myself. It's not only *my* future that's at stake.'

'If you were certain of your feelings for Terry, surely you wouldn't have any doubts, about him, or about Gemma's welfare?'

'When we got engaged I was certain,' Venna told her friend. 'But just lately we've begun to argue about other things besides Gemma. Uncle Lionel and I went through Terry's account books before I went into partnership with him, and at that time he seemed pretty sound financially. But... Oh, well!' Her customary optimism reasserted itself. 'I'm sure it'll sort itself out. And that's enough of my problems. I don't know what's got into me today. I don't usually go on at this length. You look tired, Carol,' she noted suddenly.

'I've had a rotten headache nearly all day,' the older woman admitted.

'Is there anything I can do for you?' Venna was immediately concerned.

'Heavens!' Carol laughed. 'You've enough to do without bothering about me. But thanks all the same.'

'Come on, Gemma, poppet.' Venna stood up. 'Time we weren't here. Auntie Carol's tired. Thanks for the tea, Carol, and the chat.' Penitently, 'You shouldn't have let me go on bending your ear with my life story and my problems. It's just that there isn't really anyone else I can talk to about something that concerns Gemma. Only you and Terry know the truth about her—and the aunts, of course. But they wouldn't be much help.' Not even Carol's husband was party to the secret.

'You can talk to me any time,' the older woman said warmly. 'If it helps you, I'm always ready to listen.'

Mothers were arriving to collect their offspring, and as Venna dressed Gemma in her outdoor things she thought how different their circumstances were. For the most part the other children would be returning to family homes, to older brothers and sisters, in most cases a father.

As she drove along tree-lined Lord Street in the direction of home, Carol's remarks about Shelagh repeated themselves over and over in her mind to the rhythm of the tyres swishing on the wet road surface. In imagination Venna was back in the past, nearly three years ago, that other cold, wet March day, when Shelagh had made that shocking announcement. 'Vee, I've decided to have a baby.'

'You're pregnant?' Venna had asked incredulously.

'No, but if I get my way I soon will be.'

At first Venna had laughed disbelievingly. It was a joke. It must be. The half-sisters shared a quirky sense of humour inherited from their beautiful, fun-loving mother.

'How on earth can you have a baby when you're not even married?'

The half-sisters lived a long way apart. Since she had qualified as a solicitor, Shelagh lived and worked in London. Acting on her great-uncle Lionel's advice, Venna had only recently moved from Preston to Southport. But they wrote and visited each other regularly, and as far as Venna knew Shelagh hadn't even got a man in her life right at that moment. She'd had one or two boyfriends, but Venna was almost certain her half-sister had never been intimate with any of them. She felt sure Shelagh wasn't promiscuous by nature. Neither had she shown any signs of wanting to marry any of her menfriends. Equally, none of them apparently wanted to marry her.

'You're not that naïve, Vee,' Shelagh said lightly. 'It's quite easy to have a baby. You don't have to be married.'

When Venna realised Shelagh was serious, she told her not to be so stupid. How did she think she was going to look after a baby when she had such a demanding job? She might as well have saved her breath. Another trait the half-sisters shared was stubbornness.

'I want a baby,' Shelagh asserted. 'You know I've always wanted one, and I'm going to have one.' She would, she argued, make a perfectly good mother. She didn't see what difference being married made. 'It's no good you looking shocked, young Vee, and don't go on about Granny Birtles turning in her grave. It just so happens that I agree with the things she used to say. No man is going to get a chance to make me miserable.'

'But what about the great-aunts? What on earth are they going to say about you being an unmarried mother?'

'Blow the great-aunts. They've never approved of me, anyway. You were always their favourite. The truth of it is, they'll probably be madly jealous. None of them ever had kids. And the expression unmarried mother is out,' Shelagh went on. 'We're called single parents these days. We're an accepted section of society.'

'But how are you going to...?'

'Oh, I'll find someone to oblige,' Shelagh interrupted airily.

Against Venna's strenuous objections Shelagh had employed all the usual feminist arguments. What was the difference between her idea, Shelagh demanded, and that of married women who sought artificial insemination by an anonymous donor?

Venna had tried everything. If Shelagh was so set against conventional marriage, couldn't she at least live with the father? That would be something. At least she would have moral and financial support. How would she cope on her own with pregnancy? And afterwards, if she was ill, who would look after the child?

'A baby isn't a doll, you know. It needs a lot of attention.'

'I've got plenty of friends who'll come to the rescue,' Shelagh asserted confidently.

'But what about your job?' Venna protested. Shelagh had only qualified as a solicitor a year ago.

'There are such things as day nurseries. There's no reason these days why mothers shouldn't have careers.'

'But you'll miss all the fun of your baby growing up.'

'There'll be evenings and weekends. You're too cautious, young Vee. You can't always be thinking "what if". As you said, the great-aunts will huff and puff, but I thought you at least would sympathise. We've always been good friends and you're always saying you'd like a family yourself.'

'Yes, but I plan to get married first,' Venna said firmly. But Shelagh had touched on her weak point, if it could be called a weakness. Despite Venna's disapproval of her half-sister's plans, she loved Shelagh and whatever she did would certainly never let her lack for help or support.

Time passed and nothing more was said either in their letters or during visits, and Venna hoped Shelagh had forgotten her crazy idea. Professionally her half-sister seemed to be very busy, and she was leading her normal social life. Then, some months later, Shelagh arrived on Venna's doorstep to tell her she was pregnant. She was so ecstatically happy that Venna hadn't the heart to criticise.

'Who...? Do you know who the father is?' she asked.

'Of course I do!' Shelagh was indignant. 'What do you take me for? Oh, it's no one you know. Just someone I met on holiday this year.' Shelagh had spent a month supposedly touring the West Country.

'You just went and picked up some strange man, had an...an affair with him? You weren't even in love with him or anything?'

'I don't think I know what you mean by love.' Shelagh was quite serious. 'He was very attractive. I liked him. I wouldn't have picked just anyone to father my child. He was intelligent too, and healthy.'

'And what about him? Did he realise...? Or...? I mean did you *tell* him?'

'Oh, I think he believed it was going to be a grand romance. He even said he was in love with me. But I made it quite clear to him when I said goodbye that I meant just that.'

'But if he thought he was in love with you, he must have been terribly hurt!' the tender-hearted Venna exclaimed. 'Won't he come looking for you?'

'I didn't tell him where I lived, or give him my real name,' Shelagh explained.

'What did you call yourself?' Venna still couldn't approve, but she had to admit her stepsister's thoroughness.

'Oh, nothing way-out. Just the first name that came into my head when he asked me, and no surname.'

Despite Shelagh's airy self-confidence, Venna had worried about the older girl going back to London alone. At that time Venna had been too busy to have made many close friends in Southport, and those she had made in Preston during her schooldays had married or moved on, scattered to the four winds. Her friendship with Carol Wood was of too recent a date at that time and she didn't relish telling her great-aunts about Shelagh's pregnancy. With no one else to confide in, she had discussed the matter with her partner. Terry Little was openly disgusted.

'Your half-sister obviously has no respect for men. She's just used some poor devil as... as a stud. She talks about women's rights. What about the father's rights?'

Though privately Venna agreed with him, she found herself loyally defending Shelagh's right to live her life her own way.

None of Venna's pessimistic forecasts came true. Shelagh sailed through her pregnancy without any of its attendant problems. She had no morning sickness, no high blood-pressure. She even began to talk about having a second child in the same way. In fact, she had worked up to within a week of Gemma's birth. The firm of solicitors had been very good about maternity leave, and when Shelagh returned to work baby Gemma had been deposited daily at a nursery.

Venna had visited her half-sister as often as she could be spared from the bookshop, and was present when Gemma was born. Though she could still not approve of her half-sister's actions, Shelagh proved to be, as Venna had known she would be, an extremely efficient as well as a doting mother, the baby's routine fitting successfully into her life-style. Venna tried to visit more regularly, and grew more and more fond of her baby niece.

Then, only months later, the only eventuality Venna hadn't foreseen occurred—the horrific six-vehicle pile-up that had killed her half-sister outright. The friends Shelagh had so blithely spoken of declared themselves quite unable to offer help. Venna wasn't really surprised by this. But, in any case, as Gemma's godmother and aunt she considered it only right that she should look after Gemma. But it wasn't just duty that prompted her. It was a question of love.

By this time she was engaged to Terry. Her fiancé had been strongly in favour of baby Gemma being put up for adoption. But Venna wouldn't hear of it. And when Terry muttered about Shelagh's irresponsible behaviour she reminded him, 'Even if Shelagh had been married to Gemma's father, she and her husband could have both been killed in a car crash. The result would have been just the same.'

'The husband would have had family,' Terry said.

'Not necessarily,' Venna argued, and there the matter had rested uneasily for just over a year. But lately Terry had been complaining, not without justification, Venna admitted, that it was about time they got married.

Baby Gemma was the cause of dissension between them yet again, next morning, when Venna arrived at the tall side-street shop, accompanied by her small niece.

'You're late!' Terry Little greeted her, arms aggressively akimbo. 'And what's the child doing here?'

'Carol Wood's gone down with 'flu,' Venna explained. 'She was feeling lousy yesterday. Her husband phoned this morning to put me off. Gemma won't be any trouble, Terry,' she promised hastily as his frown deepened. 'She's very well behaved.'

'She'd better be. I don't want to find sticky finger-marks on my stock.'

'*Our* stock!' Venna reminded him quietly but pointedly.

'Talking of which,' Terry went on, 'I've unloaded those books I bought yesterday. You might sort them and price them today, and get them on the shelves.'

'Why? Where will you be?' Venna asked.

'I've heard there's a chap up in Windermere who's retiring and disposing of his stock. I thought I'd take a run up there and see if there's anything worth having.'

'Terry, we ought not to buy any more books just yet. You spent an awful lot yesterday.'

'Don't start on that again!' Terry warned. 'Anyway, I haven't got time to argue. Now you're finally in, I'm off. And don't complain about having to cope single-handed. You're the one who's always saying we can't afford an assistant.'

'I wasn't going to complain,' Venna said with dignity. 'I'm quite capable.'

'And it's not *my* fault,' Terry went on, 'that you're saddled with the kid as well.'

Venna bit back a sharp retort as she watched Terry's short, slight figure disappear through the door. As she turned to survey the task before her she sighed a little despondently. It wasn't the thought of the busy day ahead that dismayed her. She had been a bookworm all her life and usually she enjoyed her work. Normally she relished the opportunity of dipping between the covers as she sorted and stacked new volumes on the shelves.

No, it was her relationship with Terry that was worrying her. It wasn't just their disagreements over Gemma. As she had told Carol, other irritants were beginning to creep in. More than ever she was beginning to think marriage between them could be a disaster. But if she were to break off their engagement, what about their business partnership? It was a mistake, she had begun to realise, to let emotional involvements creep into working relationships.

The side-street bookshop was an old, five-storey building, tall and rambling. The ground floor was devoted to a small office and the shop where new books were displayed. On the next floor were the more expensive antiquarian and collectors' items. The remaining floors held the cheaper second-hand stock. Despite all Venna's efforts at organisation, books overflowed from the various rooms and lay in piles down either side of the narrow staircases, leaving room for only one person at a time to ascend or descend.

In the office a cheerful fire burned in the old-fashioned grate, and Venna checked that the fireguard was safely in place before settling Gemma on the rug with her toys. This done, she made a random selection from the dozens of cardboard boxes stacked beside the desk and began to inspect the contents.

As she worked she had to admit that there were some very choice items among Terry's purchases. But because he had paid so much for them, the mark-up would be very small and it might be months, even years, before they all sold. It would be a good idea, she thought, to update the catalogue they sent out to selected customers and include these new titles. Normally the catalogue was revised six-monthly, but it would be worth the outlay on postage to try to recoup some money. She hoped fer-

vently that Terry would not spend too much today in
Windermere.

From time to time she glanced through the office
window into the shop. In the years since they had opened
the shop they hadn't had any trouble with pilfering, but
it was as well to be alert to the possibility. During the
first hour two or three people wandered in, browsed for
a while, then left without making any purchase. Apart
from keeping a weather eye on them, Venna left them
to their own devices. If customers appeared to need as-
sistance she would go out into the shop.

The afternoon was busier, but even so she was delving
into the last box of books when she heard the shop bell
clang. She looked up to make her usual brief assessment
of the newcomer, then, her attention riveted, found
herself unable to look away. He was the kind of man
who certainly warranted a prolonged inspection, a
second, even a third look.

The rooms of the old bookshop were high-ceilinged,
and usually customers appeared dwarfed by the proportions. Not so this man. He was all of six feet and
more, Venna guessed. Not only tall, but broad and
powerfully built. Even at this distance Venna was con-
scious of the virility he emanated. He had a large, strong
head covered in blue-black hair, a lot of it, in well-cut
layers. He wore impeccably tailored trousers and a duffel
coat beneath which a white sweater emphasised his
swarthy complexion. Unlike most customers he did not
go straight to the shelves, but stood looking about him.
But only for the length of time it had taken Venna to
make this brief appraisal of his appearance. The next
instant he strode purposefully towards the office. He had
a slight limp, she noticed, but it didn't seem to reduce
the speed of his impatient, forceful stride. He was just
another customer and yet, as he approached, Venna was
aware that the rate of her heartbeat had increased.

The office door had been closed to prevent Gemma straying, and now it was flung open without even the ceremony of a preliminary knock.

'Can I help you?' Venna asked. She was still strangely uneasy and not a little annoyed by his invasion of the private office, but her customary courtesy did not desert her. She pushed back her chair and stood up.

Seen closer, the man's dark head had greying temples that betrayed his age—approaching forty, she would have said. Thick, straight eyebrows were as dark as his hair, and at the moment they were drawn together over grey eyes that for some reason struck a chill in Venna as they surveyed her. It was a comprehensive stare that took in her slight form in its workaday uniform of jeans and the sweater which emphasised rather than concealed her slender but seductive curves.

'Well, Venna, so I've found you at last!' His voice was deep and should have been a pleasant one, but he gave a cutting edge to his words.

'I'm sorry.' Venna was puzzled. 'I don't quite...'

'No? Perhaps you don't. But you soon will.' He looked about him, the grey eyes taking in the room's shabby comfort, the overspill of books. Then, as his inspection reached the child playing on the floor, his expression became, if anything, more grim.

'Yours?' he snapped out the question.

'Yes. That is...'

'So-o!' It was a long-drawn-out exhalation of breath. 'How old?' His mouth was a taut line.

'Eighteen months, but...' Venna had been about to ask him what his interest was, to ask him to declare his business. But she broke off and watched incredulously as he moved towards Gemma, then actually swooped and picked her up. He held the child aloft, staring into the solemn little face. Gemma in turn regarded him with no sign of fear, then gave him one of her most engaging, dimpled grins. She had never been given cause to fear anyone, man or woman.

Venna saw the startled expression that for an instant shattered the inscrutable stoniness of his face, making it come alive, making her suddenly tinglingly aware of his attraction. For, though there was something about him, apart from his behaviour, that made her feel oddly antagonistic, he *was* attractive. Not handsome, she decided. His features were too blunt and craggy for that. But his face was an interesting one, and belonged to a man who looked as though he could probably be ruthless on occasion. He was dark-complexioned, almost as though he had a built-in tan that lasted all year round.

'Good God! It's quite incredible!'

'What is?' Venna had begun by being annoyed by his manner, his almost rude intrusion. Now she was curious, but also a little anxious. After all, she and Gemma were alone here, and not many people came into the shop this near to closing time. She wasn't normally nervous, but somehow this large man seemed to represent a threat to her peace of mind.

'At least she's nothing like you!' The man sounded as if the fact were a matter for satisfaction, and Venna felt a moment of pique, though she hardly knew why. It wasn't as if she had ever been vain about her own appearance.

'No,' she agreed, concealing the chagrin. The remark was often made to her, since everyone believed Gemma to be her child. 'She's not.'

Where Venna and Shelagh, like their late mother, had both been green-eyed redheads, Gemma was silky fair with enormous brown eyes which added to an air of solemnity almost unnatural in so young a child. Venna had long since come to the conclusion that Gemma must resemble her unknown father.

To Venna's relief the man put Gemma down, but she became uneasy again when the grey eyes returned to their comprehensive assessment of *her*. Her heart, she realised, was fluttering in her breast like a captive butterfly. And his silvery gaze seemed to impale her as though she were just such an unfortunate insect.

'It was a clever plan, Venna,' he drawled, 'but not quite clever enough. Did you really think you could hide for ever in a country the size of England? You should have gone abroad. You might have stood a chance then. You might even have got away with it if you'd given a false name. If my work didn't take me abroad a lot of the time I'd have been calling on you even sooner.' He looked down at Gemma again. 'I'd rather suspected I might find this little bonus, and it seems I was right.'

Venna's mouth had gone dry and she felt her knees begin to shake. She was quick-witted and intelligent, and it hadn't taken long for this last speech of his to register, for her to put two and two together. Especially when he had mentioned the use of a false name. Shelagh had been very evasive about the pseudonym she had given to the man who had fathered her child. No wonder! For now Venna knew why. The first name that had sprung into Shelagh's mind had been hers. Her half-sister had called herself Venna. And this... Venna sat down suddenly. This must be Gemma's father.

But immediately upon this thought came incredulity. Venna and her stepsister had been very much alike in build and colouring, though Shelagh had been a little taller. But it wasn't as if they were twins. Venna felt herself beginning to blush. How could a man who had been on such terms of intimacy with her half-sister mistake her for Shelagh? Surely it just wasn't possible? Her conjectures were interrupted by the man's impatient voice, his words confounding her.

'You don't know me, of course. Let me introduce myself. Keir Trevelyan.' And, as she stared blankly at him, her thoughts still on her stepsister's imposture, 'The name doesn't ring a bell? Doesn't mean anything to you?'

Again he made an almost insolent inventory of her appearance. 'Somehow you're not quite what I expected, in spite of the photographs.'

'Photographs?' Venna asked, dry-mouthed. Shelagh hadn't mentioned anything about photographs.

'You wouldn't know about those, of course. Tris said you were camera-shy. Apparently he took them with a telescopic lens, when you weren't looking. Poor besotted fool.' Now he sounded sad as well as angry.

'Tris?'

'Oh, come now, Venna!' Once more anger was uppermost, a kind of savage anger. 'Don't try to pretend you've forgotten Tris. Tristram Trevelyan, my brother, and now, I discover, the father of your child.'

Venna's first impulse was to deny it, to blurt out the truth. The words were actually on her lips. But something made her bite them back. Some primitive instinct of caution told her it might not be wise to disclose that Gemma wasn't her child.

'Oh, *that* Tris,' she said quickly, then realised immediately how idiotic the remark must sound.

'You know so many?' Keir Trevelyan sounded scornfully disbelieving.

'What I meant was,' she improvised, 'I'd forgotten that was his name.' It was the wrong thing to say. Venna realised that immediately as his thick eyebrows elevated almost to his hairline. But she hadn't exactly had time to think of something more credible, she thought crossly.

'You'd *forgotten* his name?' Keir Trevelyan was even more angry and coldly contemptuous. 'Well, I suppose that figures. I suppose I should be surprised instead that you even bothered to ask it. You promiscuous little tramp!' It was her late half-sister he was castigating. Venna knew that, but he didn't. Even so, she found his manner extreme.

'Now hold on!' she exploded. She was on her feet again, eyes blazing. 'Don't you talk to me like that. You

march into my private office without so much as a by
your leave and...'

'Leave out the righteous indignation!' The contempt
was weary now. 'It doesn't cut any ice with me. I'm the
one with the grievance. I've spent a lot of money having
you tracked down.'

'I can't think why,' she retorted.

'Believe me, on my own account I wouldn't have done.'

'Then why?'

'Because,' he grated, 'my poor bloody brother killed
himself because of you. Because he suspected he might
have fathered a child. Because I promised him I'd find
you, no matter how long or what it took to do so.'

'Your—your brother killed himself.' Venna had the
pale skin that often accompanied red hair. But now she
blanched still further, throwing into relief the light
dusting of freckles on nose and cheeks.

'Oh, don't flatter yourself it was deliberate.' Keir
Trevelyan's tone was biting. 'Tris was cut up about the
way you treated him, but he was no weakling. He drove
here and there all over the country every moment he
could spare, looking for you, until one day on a particularly long trip he crashed his car on the motorway. He
survived a couple of days. Just long enough to tell me
what little he knew about you and to extract a promise
from me.'

'I'm—I'm sorry.' Venna meant it. She had a soft heart,
but in any case she had always felt sorry for the man
Shelagh had used so cavalierly. Now she thought of his
unhappiness. He must have loved her stepsister to search
for her so diligently. And then to be killed doing so...
Her lips quivered. She blinked back tears, but they had
not gone unobserved.

'Tears? Crocodile tears!' her accuser jeered. 'Don't
try and pretend to me that you have any feeling for my
poor unfortunate brother. You weren't in love with him.

Or so you told him. You told him you didn't believe in love.'

She faced him resolutely, chin tilted, her eyes still over-bright.

'Mr Trevelyan, you can think what you like, but I *am* very sorry to hear of your brother's death.'

Venna had never thought too much of her own appearance. Though her features were regular, she considered her face to be a little on the long side, her mouth too large, her nose too tip-tilted. Her eyes, she allowed, were her best feature, startlingly green, immense, widely spaced, fringed by long, sooty lashes. But at that moment of heightened emotion she was beautiful. Her face was luminous, its pallor intensified by the lustrous wine colour of her hair. Her mouth was all compassionate curves, while her eyes betrayed the intensity of her feelings.

'You should have been an actress, Venna.' In contrast to his earlier angry tones, Keir Trevelyan's voice sounded strangely husky. 'If I didn't know better, I'd find myself believing you.'

There was a long, almost tense silence in which grey eyes held green, and something nameless, intangible, stretched between man and woman. It was a relief to Venna when finally the silence was broken by Gemma. She had almost forgotten her niece's presence, Venna thought wonderingly.

'Mummy?' Gemma had only just learned the word when Shelagh was killed. Now, Venna reflected, it was just as well she hadn't discouraged the child from calling *her* 'mummy' instead. 'Mummy! Dwink!'

'This is hardly the place for a small child,' Keir Trevelyan said critically as Venna took milk from the office refrigerator and poured a glass for her niece.

'She isn't always here.' Venna was immediately on the defensive. 'I have a friend who usually looks after her.

Not that it's any business of yours,' she remembered somewhat belatedly.

'I disagree. She's my niece.'

'You can't be sure of that,' Venna fenced. She had already realised that when it came to blood relationship, Keir Trevelyan had as much claim to baby Gemma as she, and fear gripped her. But he couldn't, surely he wouldn't want to take Gemma away from her, she told herself.

'Normally I'd agree with you,' he said. 'With a woman of your kind, I suppose the child might have been fathered by one of a dozen. But as it happens, the likeness is too remarkable.'

'Oh! What a perfectly foul thing to say!' Venna forgot fear in indignation. 'Shel... I mean, I...' In her anger she had nearly blurted out Shelagh's name. She must be careful. She might not be Gemma's real mother, but she had been as good as. And she adored the child. To Venna, Gemma was hers now. She mustn't let Keir Trevelyan suspect the truth and perhaps risk losing the child. For the time being she would play along with his misapprehension. 'That is,' she went on, 'there wasn't anyone else. Gemma is your brother's child.' Triumphantly she played what she thought to be a trump card. 'You've just admitted she's like him.'

'No, I haven't!' Keir Trevelyan was looking at her rather oddly, Venna thought. 'When I said the likeness was remarkable, I didn't mean she was like Tris, but like my sister as a child.' Curiously, 'Didn't Tris ever tell you about Maria?'

'Er—no,' she fenced. 'I don't believe so.'

'I find that rather strange,' Keir said slowly, thoughtfully. He pushed some books aside and sat down on the edge of the desk, arms folded. 'Maria was Tris's twin. Though they weren't identical twins, they were very close. Maria died five years ago. Neither Tris nor my mother really got over it.' He looked down at Gemma, who was happily engrossed with her toys once more. The expression on his rugged features was one of satisfaction. 'This child will be a great consolation to my mother.'

'What do you mean by that?' Venna snapped suspiciously.

'I should have thought that was obvious. You don't think now I've found you, and especially now that I know there is a child, that I'm going to go quietly away and forget your existence? This child is a Trevelyan.'

'That isn't the name on her birth certificate,' Venna told him. Shelagh had refused to declare the identity of the child's father, and Gemma was registered as Gemma Redmond. Redmond had been the name of Shelagh's father. But the next moment Venna was regretting her triumphant assertion.

'Maybe, and I shall want documentary proof of that,' he confounded her by saying. 'But she's a Trevelyan, all the same,' he went on. 'She belongs to my family.'

'She belongs to me!' Venna cried agonisingly. At the very real pain in her voice Keir Trevelyan gave her another of his penetrating looks, noting for the first time her air of fragility, the transparent honesty of the large green eyes.

'You sound as if that really mattered to you!' He seemed to find it a subject for incredulity.

'It *does* matter. I *love* Gemma!' Her voice was husky with sincerity.

'And yet, judging by the way you treated Tris, I'm surprised you didn't take precautions against getting pregnant, and that you decided to keep his child. Why did you keep her, Venna?'

She drew a deep breath. She hated lies and deception, but this was where she must act—act as if her life depended on it. Gemma's future with her could be at stake. She cast her mind back to some of the things Shelagh had said.

'It was only having a child that interested me,' she told Keir Trevelyan. 'I wasn't in love with your brother.' And, defiantly at his condemnatory look, 'He was only the means to an end. I didn't want to get married—to him or to anyone. But I did want Gemma.'

'My God!' It was said disbelievingly. He stood up and looked down at her from his vastly superior height. 'I've heard of women like you, but I don't think I've actually ever met one. You really mean it, don't you?'

'Yes.' Committed now to a course of action, she had to keep up the pretence, however much she hated it.

'Of all the cold, calculating little bitches! And my brother had to fall for *you*.'

Venna shrugged, tried to look as if his contempt left her unmoved.

'And what kind of a mother do you think you are?' Keir Trevelyan demanded. 'When it's obvious you don't even know the meaning of the word love. Love isn't just a question of possession. And that's all the child is to you—a possession.'

'No!' she denied, but he persisted.

'My brother's child has a right to know where she belongs. She should be where she'll be really loved and valued—as a member of a proper family, her father's family. I want Tris's child, Venna.'

CHAPTER TWO

'WELL, you're not getting her!' Venna's mounting
anxieties coalesced into one violent explosion of anger.
With a swift, fluid movement of her slender body she
placed herself between Keir Trevelyan and Gemma. For
a moment she really feared he would attempt to snatch
the child away there and then. Tigress-like, her green
eyes dared him to try.

She was just wondering what she could do to prevent
him—he was so dauntingly large—when the shop
doorbell clanged and Terry Little entered, his slight figure
staggering under the weight of a box of books. Venna
was so relieved to see him that for the moment she forgot
to be anxious about how much money he must have
spent.

'I've got another two boxes in the van.' Terry was ju-
bilant. 'Brrr, it was bitterly cold up in the Lakes. It was
just beginning to snow when I left Windermere.' He
spared Keir Trevelyan only a cursory glance as he dumped
his burden on the floor. Then, as he straightened, he
seemed to become aware of the tension in the atmosphere, of Venna's defensive attitude. 'Something wrong,
Venna?'

'No. Mr Trevelyan was just leaving,' Venna said
pointedly.

'Oh, no, he wasn't,' Keir Trevelyan drawled. 'Not by
a long way.'

Terry assessed him. To do so he had to look up at the
other man who topped him by seven or eight inches.
Knowing Terry, Venna recognised his chagrin. He dis-

liked his lack of inches and automatically resented those who made him aware of his deficiencies.

'Are you a customer, Mr . . . ? Trevelyan, was it?'

'No, I'm not a customer, Mr . . . ?' Deliberately the tall man aped Terry's slightly pompous manner and Venna saw Terry stiffen.

'Little,' Venna supplied in an attempt to defuse the situation. 'Terry Little, my partner.'

'And her fiancé,' Terry put in as he always did, but his manner was more assertive than usual.

'*Fiancé?*' Keir Trevelyan snapped out the word and his grey eyes narrowed as he rounded abruptly on Venna. 'I thought marriage was out where you're concerned.'

'Venna? Against marriage?' Terry chipped in before she could answer. 'What utter rubbish!' Then, 'What's this all about, Venna? Who *is* this?'

'It's unlikely, I suppose, that you've told your fiancé about your chequered past,' Keir said. 'But I'm afraid the cat's out of the bag now.'

'Terry knows all about Gemma,' Venna interrupted. Her hand placed on Terry's arm exerted pressure, reminding him not to be indiscreet. 'Terry, this is Gemma's uncle. He's been trying find *me*,' she emphasised, 'for some time.'

'Uncle?' Terry stared at Keir Trevelyan. 'You mean her father, surely?'

'No,' Keir said, 'my brother is dead.'

'Then Gemma's an . . .' Terry began.

'. . . only has me,' Venna put in hastily, 'which is all she's ever had, or needs!' she concluded challengingly, her firm little chin elevated at Keir Trevelyan. He met her challenge with implacable coolness.

'And I disagree. But how about you, Mr Little, since this would seem to concern you, too? Do you really want the responsibility for another man's child? Don't you think the child would be better off with her natural father's family, the advantages they have to offer?'

'I most certainly do think so!' Terry said emphatically. 'In fact I...'

'And your fiancé's opinion must carry some weight?' Keir asked Venna.

'Yes, Venna, surely...' Terry began, but she cut in again warningly, afraid of what he might be going to say.

'I'd rather we discussed this alone, Terry, in private.' For a moment she thought he was going to argue, but then he shrugged.

'OK. I may as well bring in the rest of the books, then. Cash up, will you, Venna? It's past closing-time,' he pointed out.

'You'll have to leave now,' she told Keir Trevelyan with some satisfaction.

'Oh, no.' He shook his head. 'You don't get rid of me that easily. I'll run you home when you've finished. We can continue our discussion there.' He sounded irritatingly certain that she had no choice but to comply. When she liked, Venna could exude an icy hauteur, a dignity that belied her warm colouring and slight stature.

'I have my own transport,' she informed him. 'And I don't hand out my address to all and sundry.'

'So my brother discovered,' he observed tautly. He folded his arms across his broad chest and leant against the jamb of the door. 'You led my enquiry agents a pretty dance. But I know now where you live, Venna. So we can do this your way or mine. The hard way or the civilised way. It's your decision.'

'Civilised?' Her eyes flashed emerald fire at him. 'I suppose your idea of being civilised is for me to meekly hand Gemma over to you? Well, I shan't.'

'No,' he observed her thoughtfully, his expression momentarily less austere, 'I don't believe you will. As I said before, somehow you're not quite what I expected.' He sounded puzzled. 'That's why we need to discuss this further. I'm not an unreasonable man. Perhaps we could come to some sort of compromise.'

'Compromise?' Venna was still suspicious. 'What sort of compromise?'

'You haven't time to discuss it now,' Keir pointed out smoothly. 'You have to shut up the shop. And isn't it time that child,' he indicated a drooping Gemma, 'was at home getting ready for bed? I'll come round to your flat later. About eight o'clock?'

She couldn't say she wouldn't be in. He knew she would have to be, because of Gemma.

'It isn't convenient,' she said, annoyed with herself at the use of such a lame excuse. She had always prided herself on being competent to deal with both her professional and her private life. But somehow this man seemed to have the effect of addling her wits.

'It wasn't exactly convenient for me to have to drive hundreds of miles to see you,' he told her drily. 'But I put duty before convenience.' He straightened up, turned on his heel. 'I'll see you at eight.' He threw the words over one broad shoulder as he left. 'And don't get any ideas about not opening the door to me.'

The idea *had* crossed her mind, but she had rejected it. She was beginning to realise that Keir Trevelyan didn't take no for an answer, and she didn't want an embarrassing scene within earshot of the occupants of neighbouring flats.

She wasn't going to be ready when he came, Venna thought crossly as she dashed around the flat doing the tidying up she hadn't had time for that morning.

With Keir Trevelyan's departure, Terry made no secret of his delight that the other man was laying claim to Gemma. He obviously saw it as Venna's chance to abrogate all responsibility for her niece. Now, he urged, they could get married and the child would no longer be a cause of dissension between them.

Venna had been angry with him and they had argued for at least half an hour without coming any closer to a mutually agreeable solution. The argument had become a full-blown row until, goaded finally beyond endurance, Venna had removed her ring and with icy fury ended their engagement. Terry had accused her of making the gesture in the hope that it would persuade him to accept Gemma.

'Well, it won't work!' he'd told her. 'And you don't mean it.'

But she had meant it, Venna thought now, wearily. Her feelings were mixed—anger, but depression too at the ending of a relationship. But there was a sense of relief as well. She had done the right thing.

Then, when Venna and Gemma had finally reached home, the child was overtired and uncharacteristically cranky. Tea time, bath time and bed time seemed endlessly prolonged and, though she too was tired, Venna would not let herself become impatient with her small niece.

There was no time to cook herself a meal. Besides, she didn't feel like eating. She wasn't looking forward to the coming re-encounter with Keir Trevelyan. Ironically, Shelagh, the solicitor, would have been aware of her legal rights, able to argue them. Venna doubted whether *she* had any rights. But, in any case, she didn't want the possession of Gemma to be turned into a court case. She didn't want Gemma to become the publicised object of a tug-of-love sensation.

She was determined that her flat should present an immaculate appearance when Gemma's uncle arrived. He would be left in no doubt as to her suitability as a mother. Consequently she tidied up her own possessions and Gemma's, vacuumed and dusted, and left herself only the minimum of time to shower and change.

But what to wear? That seemed important too, though only for the sake of her own morale, of course. She discarded several outfits as being too dressy for an informal visit. Conversely, certain other clothes made her feel oddly dissatisfied with her appearance. Not that it mattered what she looked like, was her final exasperated thought. It wasn't her appearance but her character that was in question, and Keir Trevelyan had a preconceived notion of that in any case. In the end she settled for a smarter pair of jeans and an angora sweater that had miraculously escaped the attention of Gemma's often sticky fingers.

Even though she was expecting it, she jumped when the doorbell rang. She took a deep breath and presented a deliberately calm façade to the man who stood in the doorway, concealing the renewed trepidation she felt at the sight of him. The appearance of fear could weaken her position. She tried unsuccessfully to read his expression as he strode over her threshold looking taller, broader and swarthier than she remembered.

She followed him into the living-room, seeing it critically through his eyes. It wasn't luxurious, but it was clean and comfortable. The flats were a conversion from an old Victorian house overlooking Hesketh Park. The large rooms were airy and graceful. When decorating, Venna had plumped for the austerity of plain cream walls and varnished boards, softened by colourful rugs and thriving green plants. In one of the room's deep alcoves, floor-to-ceiling shelves held the books without which Venna could not live.

She stood with her back to the fireplace where an electric, coal-effect fire had replaced the old grate. Background heating was supplied by a radiator. With her hands thrust into her pockets to disguise their slight tremulousness, her stance was almost boyish. But there was no mistaking the femininity in softly rounded hips and shapely legs emphasised by her tightly clinging jeans. The pink fluffy sweater moulded and strained against her high, generous breasts which rose and fell with an agitation all her efforts could not suppress.

He hadn't changed his clothes, she noted, except that he had substituted a shirt for the thick sweater he had worn earlier. He shrugged off his duffel coat and she saw that his charcoal-grey suit was superbly tailored. Even without the heavy coat he appeared dauntingly large and muscular. She was quite alone with him here, with no likelihood of interruption. And she was aware of the aura of virile masculinity he exuded. Without warning, Venna felt a sudden odd surge of feeling that seemed to have nothing to do with her anxiety.

'Would you like a drink?' she offered, anxious to break a silence that threatened to become intense.

'No, thanks.' An impatient wave of his hand gestured to her to sit down. She had deliberately remained standing, not wanting to lose even such a small advantage. She chose a chair furthest from his and waited tensely for him to speak. But his opening gambit was not what she had expected.

'So how did you like Cornwall, Venna?'

Cornwall? Venna's quick brain clicked into gear. 'Tre', 'Pol', 'Pen', the prefixes that denoted not all, but many Cornish names. Keir Trevelyan was from Cornwall. Shelagh had holidayed in the West Country, and that must be where she had met Keir's brother.

Venna's father, though his name had been Leigh, had been a Cornishman, a chef at a hotel in Penzance. Granny Birtles had always scornfully declared that on both occasions her daughter had married beneath her. After Venna's father had deserted his little family, and until her mother's death, they had continued to live in Penzance. Venna still had a vivid, nostalgic memories of blue seas and stark grey cliffs, of sandy beaches and strident gulls that outshouted even the noisiest waves.

'I liked Cornwall very much,' she said truthfully.

'But not enough to marry my brother and live there.'
It was a statement, not a question, and Venna didn't feel
it warranted an answer. She knew so little of Shelagh's
relationship with Tristram Trevelyan, she thought,
frighteningly little. So the less she said, the better.

'What made you choose Cornwall?' he asked, and as
Venna looked questioningly at him, 'Do I have to spell
it out?' He was impatient and there was resentment, too,
in the frosty grey eyes. 'Why, with the whole world at
your disposal, did you have to pick on a Cornishman,
and my brother in particular, to sire your child?'

Venna could only guess why Shelagh had chosen
Cornwall. She suspected it might be because her half-
sister, too, had had pleasant memories of the West
Country. And she didn't actually know how Shelagh had
become acquainted with Tristram Trevelyan. But she had
to give some kind of an answer.

'Because Cornwall was far enough away to...'

'But it wasn't far enough, was it?' he reminded her
unnecessarily. Then, 'Just how well did you get to know
my brother?'

'Well enough,' she said evasively, then flushed,
thinking of the misconstruction that could be—and
was—placed on her reply.

'Evidently,' he said with deep satire, 'but that wasn't
what I meant. How much did he tell you about himself?'
His mouth twisted. It was half affectionate, reminiscent
smile, half painful grimace. 'Knowing Tris, it would be
quite a lot. Tris was a talker.'

'No,' she denied. 'He...I didn't *want* to know too
much about him. We...we didn't...' Oh, heavens, how
on earth did she bluff this out?

'You said he didn't tell you about Maria. But do you
mean to say he didn't tell you *anything* about his family?'
Keir Trevelyan sounded incredulous. 'Our long associ-
ation with Cornwall? We're very proud of that. And

what about his religious convictions, especially in view of your relationship?'

Venna, floundering in unknown waters, seized on this last.

'Religious convictions?'

'Right down through the centuries the Trevelyans have always been a deeply religious family,' Keir explained. 'And, strange as it may seem in this day and age, we continue to adhere to our notions of right and wrong. *You* may think it old-fashioned, but a Trevelyan doesn't indulge in promiscuity, and when he falls in love he marries the woman. His children bear his name and are educated in his religion. But I presume you're not a religious woman, Venna?'

'Yes, I... That is, I believe in good and evil. I don't attend any church regularly, but...'

'I see.' He sounded grim. He stood up and began to pace up and down. His large frame, his restless energy made the room seem smaller, claustrophobic. 'So my brother's child is unlikely to receive any religious instruction.'

'When she goes to school...'

'Religion needs to be inculcated from an early age. Has Gemma even been baptised?'

'There was a christening ceremony, yes. I was...' She stopped just in time. She had nearly said she'd been the godmother.

'That's something, I suppose.' He was silent for a while, but he continued his pacing and Venna watched him nervously, wondering just what line he would take next. 'When I got back to my hotel I telephoned my mother,' he said, just as the silence became unbearable. 'I told her about the child. She's naturally very excited.'

'Wasn't that a bit premature?'

'No, I don't think so.' Emphatically, 'Now that I know of Gemma's existence, I intend my mother to see her, Venna. That's what all this is about.'

'I was going to say it's a bit unfair to raise false hopes. I haven't agreed...'

'But you're going to, Venna. Don't underestimate me,' he warned. 'When I want something, I go all out to get it.' Looking at the dark, forceful face, the narrowed grey eyes, she could believe it, and a quiver of apprehension shuddered through her. She, too, was on her feet now, and she faced him doggedly.

'There's no way I...'

'There's always a way if you're determined enough. I want Gemma to be aware of her ancestry. Perhaps you don't realise how important such things are to us Cornishmen.' Suddenly his voice changed, became less frosty, almost coaxing. 'Come now, Venna, you can't deny it's reasonable for my mother to want to meet her only grandchild?'

The trouble was, Venna *couldn't* deny it. If she'd been an impartial observer of these events, she could only have supported his arguments. She had expressed her feelings on the subject to Shelagh many times.

'*Only* grandchild?' she queried.

'I'm not married.'

'Oh!' Of course, that fact didn't make any difference. Why should it? But, 'I suppose,' she said slowly, 'she could visit your mother.'

'Aah!' he exhaled on a note of satisfaction. 'Now we're beginning to get somewhere. So you do agree we have some rights?'

'I don't know that they're legal ones,' Venna said cautiously, 'but I have to admit you have natural ones. But don't think,' she warned vehemently, afraid he might think she was softening, 'that means I'd be willing to part with Gemma altogether. Try anything like that, and I warn you, I'll fight you all the way.' Her slight body was tensed as though ready for the promised battle.

'That's something that can always be discussed later,' he said evasively, filling her with new alarm. 'For the moment I'll settle for the visit, a long visit,' he emphasised.

'I can't be away from the shop for long,' she told him firmly. 'There's only Terry and me to...' Her voice trailed away as she remembered she didn't know what her future business relationship with Terry was going to be, now that their engagement was ended.

'There's no need for you to be absent from the shop. I'm quite capable of taking the child and returning her.'

'No way!' Venna's lips tightened and her eyes sparked defiance. He couldn't really think she would be naïve enough to trust him out of her sight with Gemma. 'Either I go with her, or she stays right here,' she told him firmly.

The grim look was back on his face again.

'That's something I'll have to discuss with my mother. Frankly, I don't know how she'll feel about meeting the woman responsible for her son's death.'

Venna felt the colour drain from her cheeks. She should have considered that aspect of it. How she wished this deception could have been avoided, that she could tell Keir Trevelyan the truth. Somehow, she hated the fact that this man had such a poor opinion of her. She'd had plenty of opportunity to set the record straight, of course, but she couldn't. It would destroy her claim to Gemma. She must perpetuate his belief that she was the child's mother.

'I've told you,' she said stiffly, 'I'm sorry about your brother, but I think he should take some of the blame. He was an adult. He knew what he was doing when he had an affair with... with me.' But Keir's face remained unresponsive to her plea.

'Tris didn't consider it *was* an affair. My brother fully intended to marry you. In any case,' he decided, 'it's too late to telephone my mother again tonight. I'll ring first thing in the morning and let you know her reaction. Frankly, I don't hold out much hope of her inviting you to Pednolva.'

'Pednolva?'

'Our family home. Tris didn't even mention *that*?' He shook his dark head incredulously.

Long after his departure Venna sat huddled up in her chair, deep in thought. She knew a deep sense of foreboding. Things were moving too fast. She had as good as agreed that Gemma should visit her father's family. But the visit could only lead to more complications, the necessity for more deception.

Venna didn't want to go to Cornwall posing as her half-sister. Her guardianship of Gemma was a consequence of Shelagh's unconventional behaviour. She didn't mind that. But she didn't relish the idea that anyone should think *her* capable of such behaviour. Nor did she like the idea that she might be under attack from Tristram Trevelyan's family.

Keir Trevelyan came across as an impatient man. If he returned tomorrow with an invitation from his mother, he would probably expect Venna to pack up there and then and accompany him to Cornwall. She sensed that he would not brook any delay once his plans were made.

But Venna wasn't prepared for such a precipitate course of action. If she had really been Gemma's mother, things would have been easier, but Venna needed more time to think, to prepare plausible answers to the questions that might be asked of her.

Now, if she and Gemma could get away, she brooded. If they could disappear for a few days. It would be even better, of course, if they could vanish from Keir Trevelyan's ken altogether. But Venna was realistic. Keir had declared he had spent a lot of money having her traced on just the slightest suspicion that there might be a child of his brother's affair with Shelagh. Now he knew about Gemma, Keir Trevelyan would be even more doggedly determined to track her down. No, she couldn't escape him permanently, but she could gain breathing-space and—it came to her suddenly—she knew where she could go.

She could act as quickly and decisively as Keir Trevelyan himself, she thought triumphantly as she dialled Carol Wood's number. Jim Wood answered. Carol was feeling much better, he said, but she would be out of action for a few more days.

'It's cheeky, I know,' Venna said, 'but I want to ask a favour. Carol once said if I ever wanted to get away, for a break, you had a cottage in the Lake District. Could I possibly go up there tonight, if I call round for the key?'

'Tonight?' Not unnaturally, Jim Wood sounded surprised. 'It's after eleven. Isn't that a bit late to be setting out? You're welcome to use the cottage, of course, but it's a bit primitive, and March can sometimes be a foul month up there. We only use it in summer.'

'Please,' Venna pleaded. 'I do need to get away, desperately, and I would like to go tonight.' To her relief, he didn't make any further demur.

'I'll drop the key round,' he told her, and added as she protested, 'It's no trouble. I wasn't going to bed yet.'

As soon as she had replaced the receiver, Venna went into action. She dragged out two suitcases from the flat's small box-room and filled them with clothes for herself and Gemma. She added any non-perishable foodstuffs from the kitchen cupboards. She was just about to haul them down two flights of stairs when Jim Wood arrived with the key. He insisted on helping her load the car, then hung around curiously while she got Gemma out of bed and wrapped the sleepy toddler in a blanket.

'Carol was worried when I told her you were off to the cottage. She said to ask if anything was wrong, if there was anything we could do.'

'No, thanks. Having the use of the cottage is a great help. It's just that I have some important thinking to do. Could I impose on you still further,' she asked Jim as she locked the front door, 'and leave this key with you? Could you keep an eye on the flat while I'm away?'

Venna put a hastily scribbled note through the shop door. She didn't mention the broken engagement, only that she would be in touch in a few days. As far as the shop was concerned, she felt guilty at leaving her partner in the lurch like this. She knew she should have phoned Terry, but she couldn't stand the thought of yet another argument, especially with other pressing matters on her mind.

Besides, she wanted to be on her way. Even though Keir Trevelyan wouldn't be contacting his mother for hours yet, she felt an edgy need to be as far away from him as possible. She couldn't remember ever having been this nervous in her life. She felt a superstitious, spine-chilling fear that even now he might appear and prevent her flight. But it was odd, she mused, as she took the Preston road out of Southport, her fear didn't seem to stem solely from the fact that she could lose Gemma to him. There was something else. Something unfathomable, yet which seemed to have its roots in more primitive instincts.

Forty minutes later she was through the familiar outskirts of Preston and on the motorway, heading north towards the Lake District. Venna wasn't accustomed to driving at night, and she had been tired even before she set out. When her eyelids began to droop dangerously, she stopped at a motorway service station. She didn't want to wake Gemma, so she bought coffee from a vending machine and drank it in the car. After half an hour she felt capable of driving on.

As her little car ate up the miles, she was glad of its efficient heating system, for the weather was definitely worsening, and as she turned off the motorway a few flakes of snow were beginning to fall, settling on earlier layers. She had to drive more slowly now, and dawn was breaking over the mountain peaks as she followed the winding lakeland roads and neared her destination.

The Woods' holiday cottage was situated near Coniston. Up ahead of her Venna could see the unmistakable craggy outlines of Old Man Coniston presiding benignly over his attendant fells and the alpine-like village at his feet.

One summer, years ago, Granny Birtles had taken them to Coniston for a holiday. Venna and Shelagh had climbed the Old Man, almost to the top of the venerable and dignified hump. But her route today lay not through the village on the north-western shore of Coniston Water, but on the opposite side. According to Jim Wood's instructions, a mile or so along the tree-lined road she must take an unmade, unsignposted track that swung left and up the fellside on to Forestry Commission land.

She found it without difficulty. It was a steep, narrow, curving ascent, and at one point on a hairpin bend the car's wheels skidded slightly on the snow, hard-packed by Forestry vehicles. The sight of a sheer drop on one side to the valley below made Venna catch a shaky breath.

High up on the fellside the grey-stoned, grey-slated cottage, once a farmhouse, stood in a prettily wooded site far from any other signs of habitation. Venna ran her car into the shelter of an old barn at the rear of the building, then carried the still-sleeping child into the cottage.

By the time she had returned for her luggage, snow was falling fast enough to obscure her footprints, and Venna felt a twinge of anxiety. She had escaped, at least temporarily, from Keir Trevelyan and his demands, and she wasn't far in terms of mileage from civilisation. Later in the day, when the shops opened, she would have to go down into Coniston village for supplies. But she hoped the weather wasn't going to deteriorate too drastically. Her near accident on the twisting track up to the cottage had made her realise it would be foolhardy to attempt the ascent and descent in really icy conditions.

The interior of the cottage was cold, but the Woods had installed their own generator and, brought up to be practical, Venna soon had the central heating going. It was not yet icy enough for pipes to have frozen. She filled kettles, then made up the double bed in the front bedroom, put in hot-water bottles and crept in beside Gemma to catch up on some badly needed sleep.

It was a delighted cry from Gemma that woke her some time later. She sat up in bed. The child was standing at the window, looking out.

'Snow! Mummy make snowman!' she demanded. Gemma knew all about snowmen from a book Venna had read to her recently.

'All right, darling,' Venna agreed. 'Breakfast first, though, and shopping.'

Driving cautiously, Venna negotiated the outward and return journey without incident. Coniston was still the charming place she remembered, even in winter. Above it the Old Man and Yewdale Crags made an impressive scene. The village was able to supply all her needs, and with the cottage larder and refrigerator stocked up for the week she felt more at ease in her mind and able to concentrate on amusing her small niece.

Warmly dressed, they built not one snowman but two, and Venna introduced Gemma to the delights of snowballing. They were tired but content when they went to bed that night.

Two or three days passed, but Venna was no nearer to the solution to the problem which had driven her here. Despite the cottage's isolation and the weather, there was plenty to hold their interest. Out of doors the snow was not too deep to preclude walks, forays deeper into the forest. Gemma enjoyed throwing out crumbs for foraging birds, and once Venna saw a deer pass quite close to the cottage.

Indoors there was television, radio and a wellstocked bookshelf, including some dog-eared souvenirs of the Wood children's youth. Gemma went to bed at her normal time, and Venna spent happy hours catching up on a recent bestseller. It was ironic, she thought, but part-ownership of a bookshop didn't mean she had all that much time to read.

On the fourth day of their stay Venna woke to a new intensity of light. She always slept with the bedroom curtains open, enjoying the view when she woke of snow-capped treetops. But this morning, as she looked towards the window, the trees were invisible, obscured by steadily falling snow. A complete white-out.

She leapt out of bed and was appalled to see just how many inches had fallen overnight. The heavy, sparkling blanket had levelled out and disguised the contours of the clearing that surrounded the cottage.

'We'll have to stay indoors today,' she told Gemma, thanking her lucky stars that her small niece was not a whining, questioning child.

They employed their time with domestic chores, the child delighted to feel she was helping. After lunch, Venna decided to make pastry, a task in which Gemma could share and which would keep the child happily absorbed for hours.

It was late afternoon, tea time, when they sat down to sample the results of their cooking. An unexpected sound drew Venna away from the kitchen table to the window which commanded a view of the approach to the cottage. Nothing could be seen through the blizzard, but she was sure she had heard the steady throb of an engine. A Forestry Commission vehicle perhaps, clearing the track. It was rather reassuring to know they weren't entirely cut off.

A grey outline appeared through the obscuring snow, grew nearer, took more definite shape. A Land Rover. Its wheels spun, but dealt with the weather conditions more efficiently than Venna could ever hope for from her little car.

The vehicle was definitely approaching the cottage. Presumably someone from the Commission had seen signs of occupancy and had come to enquire after her welfare. She could ask their advice about staying here, whether she ought perhaps to move down into the village. Venna went to the door. As she flung it open, piled-up snow tumbled in, followed by wind-gusted flakes the size of mothballs.

A bulky figure emerged from the Land Rover and, head bent against the swirling snow, made its way toward her.

'Hello!' Venna called cheerfully. 'Isn't this ghastly? I...' Like the snow driving against her face, the words froze on her lips. What was *he* doing here? How in heaven's name had he found her?

CHAPTER THREE

'SAVE the questions and the recriminations until we get inside!' Keir advised harshly.

A nervous Venna thought she had never seen any man look so furiously angry. Two forceful hands clamped her arms and moved her out of Keir Trevelyan's path as he limped purposefully across the threshold. He banged the door upon the blizzard conditions outside.

Her power of speech temporarily destroyed, Venna found herself following willy-nilly in his wake as he marched before her into the kitchen. Gemma was still seated at the table. For the child his expression softened momentarily into a smile which for that instant made him appear less daunting. He stood and looked around him, keen grey eyes taking in the spartan living conditions.

Indignantly Venna continued to follow him as he made a brisk tour of the cottage. He inspected the only other downstairs room, furnished with a shabby but comfortable three-piece suite. He climbed the narrow stairs to the second floor which consisted of a minuscule bathroom and two small bedrooms.

'Are you crazy or something?' he demanded as they returned to the kitchen. 'What on earth possessed you to bring the child to this primitive, out-of-the-way place, and in such atrocious weather?' He shrugged off his duffel coat. Flakes of snow still spangled the garment and the top of his dark head.

'It's not primitive,' Venna retorted. 'Not unless you're the kind who's accustomed to five-star living. We have everything we need. Light, heating, water, a telephone.'

'And if the telephone lines were down, as they well might be before long? What did you plan to do in an emergency?'

'I'm quite capable of coping with emergencies, and I brought Gemma here,' Venna went on doggedly, 'because it *was* out of the way! Out of *your* way!'

'And just how long were you reckoning to stay here?' His tone was sarcastic. 'You could scarcely stay in hiding for ever. Did you seriously think your running away would deter me?'

'No,' she said bitterly, 'I'm not naïve. I didn't think that.' From the very first she had sensed the bulldog tenacity of his character. It was there in the blunt, determined features, the big, bold nose, the square chin, the steely eyes.

'Then why waste time and effort on such a futile exercise, not to mention endangering the child—and yourself?' he added that very much as if it were an afterthought. He sounded utterly exasperated with her.

He thought her rash and inept, Venna realised. The realisation wasn't pleasant. And it wasn't true. She had thought this through very carefully before taking action. Though she hadn't a conceited bone in her body, she knew men usually liked her, found her intelligent as well as attractive.

'We weren't in any danger!' she defended. At least not until *you* arrived, she thought. It was quite ridiculous, this unnerving effect he had upon her. It wasn't fear exactly, but a tingling awareness of apprehension that increased the surge of adrenalin in her bloodstream. It made her wary and defensive, uncharacteristically unsure of herself.

'No?' The dark eyebrows lifted sardonically. 'You obviously haven't been far afield today. The track down to the road is impassable. You couldn't have reached the village, even in the direst emergency.'

'It didn't seem to stop you getting up here!' she pointed out, goaded into sarcasm.

'But then I have a suitable vehicle with chains on the wheels. A vehicle hired from the garage in Coniston.' He added a grim rider. 'I've had to leave my own car in the village.' Venna guessed that had annoyed him still further. As he spoke he made a brisk tour of the kitchen, throwing open the cupboards and the refrigerator to inspect their contents.

'It's a damned good job I brought some supplies up with me.'

'What on earth for?' Venna demanded. 'You may have a very low opinion of me, but credit me with *some* intelligence. Surely you didn't think I wouldn't have enough food to last out?'

'There's not enough for three people for several days.'

'Three people? Several days? But...' She'd quite expected that Keir would order her to pack up her belongings and Gemma's and accompany him immediately. She had been prepared to argue, to resist, physically if necessary. But now it sounded almost as if he intended they should all stay here together. She must have misunderstood.

'It's going to be all of that, perhaps longer, before we get out of this place,' he told her, and he sounded as if the prospect caused him distinct displeasure. That displeasure was expressed as he went on, 'I've already expended a considerable amount of valuable time in the past week—and now there's this further delay to contend with!' He indicated their surroundings, the forbidding weather outside.

'But if you got up here, surely we can...?'

'It took me two hours. In normal weather it would have taken ten minutes at the most. There's no way we're attempting the descent until this weather clears.'

And it might not clear for ages, Venna thought with a sinking feeling in her stomach. The idea of being alone at the cottage with Gemma hadn't dismayed her at all. She was normally quite self-reliant. But to be here for days, perhaps weeks, with Keir Trevelyan, was an illogically terrifying prospect. After all, he couldn't do her any harm. And if he couldn't leave here, neither could he snatch Gemma away from her, she comforted herself.

Keir made several trips through thigh-deep snow to the Land Rover, to return with heavily laden cardboard boxes. He had even brought two spare canisters of Calor gas, Venna noted. And there was enough tinned and packaged food in the boxes to withstand a long siege. Her spirits sank proportionately. He hadn't been exaggerating his concern about the weather.

The discovery that they were in for a long spell of each other's company had driven an important question from her mind. Now she asked, 'How did you know where to find us?' Her brief note hadn't told Terry where she was going.

'After two or three fruitless visits——' the irritation this had caused him was there in his deep voice '—I met some chap coming out of your flat. Your landlord, I gathered. And this cottage is his property, too. In view of the weather forecasts he was worried about you, and extremely glad, I can tell you, to hand the responsibility over to me.'

Of course. She should have known when she saw the Calor gas that Keir Trevelyan was well briefed about his destination. Fool, she adjured herself. She should have warned Jim Wood not to reveal her whereabouts to anyone in any circumstances. But she had left Southport in such a hurry.

'Altogether, Venna Leigh, you've caused me a considerable amount of inconvenience.'

'I hope you don't expect me to apologise,' she said tartly. 'I didn't ask you to meddle in my affairs.'

He didn't seem to think the remark worthy of a reply. Instead he set about opening a large tin, put a saucepan on the stove and coolly proceeded to cook himself a meal. At least he hadn't automatically expected her to wait on him, Venna thought, unwilling to grant him even that many points.

'I haven't eaten since breakfast time,' he explained, 'and that seems a very long time ago.'

She felt a pang of guilt, but feigned an indifferent shrug.

'It's time I gave Gemma her bath and put her to bed.'

'Right. When you've done that, we're going to have a talk.' He made it sound decidedly ominous, and Venna's manner as she undressed and bathed her small niece was more than a little *distraite*. So much so that the child had to voice an indignant reminder about a bed-time story.

Keir Trevelyan had made himself very much at home, Venna observed wryly when she returned downstairs. He'd eaten and washed up. Now his broad, powerful body was sprawled in one of the living-room's two easy chairs. He was leafing through some papers taken from the briefcase on the floor beside him. As Venna entered the room, he stuffed the papers away.

'Those will just have to wait—yet again,' he said with an air of weariness, and indeed he did look tired, Venna thought with an unwanted stab of compunction. But it was his fault, not hers, that he had driven all this way in such appalling conditions, she told herself, even as she noted the dark shadows under his eyes.

He was a man who needed to shave twice a day, and his jawline was blue-shadowed with the virile growth. She remembered how, by comparison, Terry's blond good looks had seemed insipid. Quite unconsciously she found herself wondering if the dark, vital hair extended to the rest of Keir Trevelyan's body, then blushed hotly at her wayward thoughts. She wasn't in the habit of indulging in such intimate conjectures about men.

'Don't mind me if you've got some work to do,' she told him. She wasn't eager to hear what he had to say, and his full, rather sensual mouth thinned into a wry smile as he recognised the ploy.

'Since I'm unlikely to be in my office for several days it makes little difference. It's more important to get Gemma's future sorted out.' Before Venna could interrupt him, he went on, 'I didn't telephone my mother again. On reflection, I decided it would only cause her unnecessary distress to meet the woman who'd caused Tris's death.'

'Gemma's not going anywhere without me,' Venna interrupted.

'If you come to Pednolva,' he stated flatly, 'you come as the child's nanny.'

And thus fog the issue of her claim to Gemma? Oh, no.

'I can't agree to that, either.'

'Don't tell me you have scruples about the masquerade,' he said sardonically. 'Not after the dance you led poor Tris.'

Venna flushed to the roots of her wine-red hair. She was already masquerading, if he only knew it. Succinctly she explained her reasons.

'How do I know it's not some trick to take Gemma away from me? Besides, Mrs Trevelyan is bound to ask what happened to Gemma's mother. What am I supposed to tell her?' she demanded. 'Even to spare her feelings, I won't live a tissue of lies.' But inwardly her conscience was deriding her necessary but unpleasant hypocrisy. How she loathed all forms of deceit!

'No, I suppose I should have expected that. After all, if you'd had any concern for other people's feelings you wouldn't have made use of Tris the way you did.' He stared at her, his grey eyes angry, then involuntarily he yawned. 'I'm tired. Too tired to argue with you any more tonight. There'll be plenty of time for that,' he reminded her unnecessarily. He stretched his arms above his head, yawned again, and with unwilling fascination Venna noted the breadth and muscularity of his chest and shoulders. He exuded such strength and masculinity and—yes—sexuality that oozed from every pore. If they had met under different circumstances, she thought a little sadly, she might have rather fancied him. Even as it was, she found him decidedly disturbing to her senses. If Tristram Trevelyan had been anything like his brother, she wondered Shelagh had been able to resist him. But she was reluctant to admit her own fascination, even to herself.

'I'll make up the other bed for you.' Anything to distract her from the sudden, unexpected surge of attraction she had felt just then. She had no need for any more complications in her life. But she was acting out of character, she realised as he raised his eyebrows—at least, out of character as *he* saw it.

'Don't bother,' he drawled. 'Just tell me where the sheets are kept and I'll do it myself. With your liberated views, I'm quite sure you don't believe in waiting hand and foot on the male sex. Incidentally, does that poor long-haired sap you're engaged to know what sort of life he's letting himself in for?'

In assuming the persona of her dead half-sister, she had also taken on the difficult and distasteful task of embodying Shelagh's cavalier attitude towards life and men. Inwardly, Venna flinched. Outwardly, she shrugged and ignored his question.

'Suit yourself!' she told him. 'The sheets are in the bathroom airing-cupboard.' She turned on her heel. 'Goodnight, Mr Trevelyan.'

'Oh, I think you'd better call me Keir, don't you, Venna? After all, we're going to be spending quite some time together.' He smiled mockingly as she failed to hide her dismay. 'We'll soon know each other far too well for such formality.'

* * *

Venna woke early after a restless night full of troubled dreams in which Keir Trevelyan snatched Gemma away from her and no matter how far or fast she travelled she could never catch up.

Immediately she was aware of a drastic change in the temperature. Because it had its own generator the cottage had been warm even on these cold March mornings. Now the bedroom she and Gemma shared was icy. Fern-like formations frosted the inside of the window-panes.

She leapt out of bed and dressed, donning an extra sweater. Then made sure the child was still snugly tucked in before going downstairs.

Early as it was, Keir must already be up. The kettle on the gas stove was still hot. But Venna had other things besides tea or coffee on her mind. She pulled on her wellingtons and opened the back door, intending to go around the side of the cottage to the generator shed.

Keir had had the same idea. A path had already been cleared. The shed door was open. Keir was bent over the generator. At the sound of her boots squeaking on the frozen surface of the snow, he looked up.

'It's packed up,' he told her grimly. 'And I can't fix it without a new part.'

'That means no central heating,' Venna was dismayed.

'Tough,' he said unsympathetically. 'You should have considered that possibility before you came chasing up here in the depths of winter. As independent as you claim to be, I don't suppose you're really used to roughing it.'

'I don't mind for myself,' Venna snapped. 'It's Gemma I'm thinking of.'

'It's a bit late for that, too. Where *is* the child?' He looked beyond her. As if, she thought indignantly, she would have dragged Gemma out here in this bitter cold.

'Still in bed, of course.' Then, 'Couldn't we get the spare part, if one of us walked down to Coniston? I know it would be hard going but . . .'

'And even if we could get the part in the village, whom did you have in mind for the errand?' he enquired. 'Some of those drifts out there are ten feet deep.'

For the first time that morning Venna looked beyond the immediate environs of the cottage at an arctic treacherous world gripped in the savagery of midwinter. Snow was still falling thickly, and searing freak winds were blowing it off the fells down into the valleys below. Apart from the eerie sound of the wind it was a silent world. Even the chatter of the nearby beck was stilled. No birds moved or called.

Her heart sank. Keir was right. No one could leave in these conditions. Not even his size and strength would be a match for such weather.

'What shall we do, Keir?' she appealed. She didn't realise that it was the first time she had used his name. But she acknowledged that it was the first time since his arrival that she'd been glad of his presence.

'Pray that the chimneys aren't blocked up,' he said with an upward glance at the cottage roof. 'There's a fuel store round the back, mainly logs. We'll carry as much as we can inside.'

With both of them working, it still took over an hour to carry all the wood into the cottage. Even though Keir had cleared a path, it was difficult to keep their feet. There was no sand or grit to scatter on the already frozen surface.

Venna worked doggedly, determined to do her share of the labour, to prove herself capable. She found it strangely enjoyable too, working side by side with Keir. They seldom spoke. But somehow the silence was a companionable one.

She didn't realise just how cold and tired she was until, her final load dumped on the kitchen floor, she straightened and swayed dizzily. Only Keir's lightning reactions saved her from a fall.

'What's wrong?' he demanded harshly as she leant briefly on his strength, a strand of her red hair brushing his cheek.

'Nothing. I just felt giddy for a moment.' He was still holding her arm. His grip, even through the two layers of sweaters she wore, was steely hard, painful. He was so close, she could smell the masculinity of him. It was curiously pleasant, a fragrance compounded of soap, the wool of his sweater and the perspiration caused by his labours. She felt her head swim again, but this time it wasn't the faintness caused by hunger and exertion. It was her sudden awareness of his male attraction, and she could not repress the little shiver that ran through her. Hastily she freed herself.

'You haven't had anything to eat this morning,' he accused. She hadn't, Venna realised. She'd been too concerned about the lack of heating to think about food. 'Sit down!' he commanded. He thrust her on to a chair, then, 'Coffee? Until I get the fire going I can't offer you toast, I'm afraid. Will a marmalade sandwich do? Or I could do bacon and egg on the Calor gas stove.'

'A sandwich will do, that is...' She struggled to rise. 'I'll make it myself.'

'You'll stay where you are. You're as weak as a kitten.' His manner was brusquely kind. But then he ruined it by adding, 'Perhaps now you're beginning to realise how foolhardy it was to run off like that, to a place like this. If I hadn't reached here when I did...'

'I don't normally forget to eat. And you seem to forget,' she pointed out, her spirit returning with her strength, 'that if it weren't for you, Gemma and I wouldn't even *be* here.'

But all the same she sipped gratefully at the coffee and munched the sandwiches he made. Meanwhile Keir investigated the condition of the living-room chimney.

'It seems all right,' he told Venna a while later. 'Before I lit the fire I poked about with a stick as far as I could reach, and I couldn't feel obstructions. Anyway, we had to risk it. The fire's caught now so you can bring the child down and feed her. Then I'll give you a hand with the bedding. Good thing I brought sleeping-bags.'

'Bedding?' she queried with a puzzled frown. 'Sleeping-bags?'

'We'll all be sleeping in there.' He jerked his head towards the living-room, from which came the cheerful sound of crackling flames. And, impatiently, as she parted her lips to expostulate, he added, 'Don't waste time arguing. There are no fireplaces in the bedrooms, and even if there were we'd still have to conserve our fuel.'

In thoughtful silence Venna went upstairs to fetch Gemma. She had to admit that everything Keir said made sense, but the idea of living *and* sleeping in quite such close proximity to him for an indefinite period was decidedly daunting.

It was bitterly cold now in the bedroom. Venna decided to dress the child downstairs in front of the fire. She was aware of Keir's eyes, keen and observant, fixed meditatively on her and on the child.

There had been an added poignancy in caring for Gemma's needs these last few days. And a fierce love filled Venna's heart now as she contemplated the unacceptable idea that she could ever lose her little niece to this man and his unknown family. Whatever it took, she resolved, she and Gemma were going to remain together. Yes, even if Keir Trevelyan insisted on her posing as Gemma's nanny. After all, the deception had been his idea, not hers, and since she was no more Gemma's mother than she was her nursemaid, one deception was no worse than the other.

She gave Gemma her cereal and a boiled egg, then left her to drink her milk while she and Keir lugged mattresses downstairs and organised the living-room furniture to fit in with their new sleeping-arrangements.

'You and the child had better be here, over against the inside wall,' Keir decided. 'I'll sleep nearest to the fire in case it needs attention during the night.'

Keir had thought of everything, Venna discovered with reluctant respect as the day wore on. He'd even brought a supply of candles, almost as if he had anticipated the breakdown in their electricity supply.

During the day, as they worked to improve their temporary accommodation, conversation was desultory, of a practical nature only. But with the onset of night, after Gemma had fallen soundly asleep, there was a sudden almost uncomfortable silence. Venna knew personalities could not be avoided much longer. Certainly her thoughts were full of the reason for their presence here, and she felt sure it wouldn't be long before Keir Trevelyan brought up the subject she dreaded.

The only light they had was that cast by the flickering flames of the fire. What a strange situation. Two virtual strangers confined by circumstances to one room. There was no outside agency to relieve their dependence upon one another for communication. With the failure of the generator there was no television, no radio. They couldn't even read. The candles were to be used only when essential.

'It must have been a bit like this in the Middle Ages,' Keir said, almost as if he had read her thoughts.

'I wonder what on earth they did,' Venna mused. She was relieved to have the uneasy silence broken by such an unthreatening topic.

'I expect they went to bed. They had pretty large families in those days.' There was a strange note in his voice, and she was glad of the semi-darkness which hid her expression as he went on, 'We won't be employing that method of passing the time.' It sounded like a warning. He couldn't think that she had imagined anything different? But she was forgetting his preconceived image of her. Honesty made her admit it was an image she'd done nothing to dispel. 'But,' he went on, 'we can sort out the matter of your visit to Cornwall, to Pednolva.'

'Oh?' Although Venna had already decided she must go along with his wishes, she wasn't going to make things too easy for him, and she remained silent apart from the non-committal sound.

'As soon as we get out of here we'll go back to Southport and pick up the rest of your things. I expect you'll want to see your partner and put him in the picture.'

'And not just Terry,' Venna put in indignantly. 'There are a lot of things I'll have to sort out if I'm going to be away for any length of time.' She bit her lip as she realised she had betrayed her acceptance of the situation.

'I'll give you two days,' he stipulated. 'And in that time I'm not letting you out of my sight.'

'Terry's not going to like it. It's very inconvenient. There's only the two of us to run the shop.'

But Keir pounced on this excuse, destroying its credibility.

'How was he supposed to manage while you were on the run? He told me he had no idea where you were. Was that the truth?'

'Yes.'

'Strange that you shouldn't want even your fiancé to know where you were,' Keir mused, a questioning note in his voice. But there was no need for him to know about the broken engagement.

'I was afraid that if he knew, he might tell you,' Venna said instead, then regretted it.

'Because he would have told me if he'd known, wouldn't he?' In the firelight she couldn't see his expression, but he sounded triumphant. 'I'd already gathered he wants to be rid of Gemma. What sort of future do you think she'd have in that kind of situation? What beats me is this. You told Tris you didn't intend to get married—ever. So how is it you got involved with

Little so soon after leaving Tris? What made you change your mind?'

'Everyone's entitled to change their mind,' she told him defensively. 'Anyway, Terry was my partner before he was my fiancé.'

'How did that come about?'

'I had some capital to invest, a legacy from my grand-mother. I'd already worked in the book trade, with my great-uncle. Terry and I had been partners for about a year when he proposed. We had a lot of shared interests, and by then we knew each other pretty well. And it was before...' She stopped short her heart thudding fear-fully. She had nearly said that was before Gemma had come into her care, which would have made nonsense of her pretence to be Gemma's mother. It just showed how difficult it was going to be to go on pretending. She might be practical and a competent businesswoman, but she just wasn't any good at lies and dissimulation.

'Have you ever slept with Little?' Keir asked bluntly, and Venna drew in a sharp, affronted breath.

'That's none of your business.' If she said 'no'—for she was still a virgin—Keir might think it strange, es-pecially in view of her supposed past. And she didn't want to say 'yes'. Even though it would be untrue, the admission would diminish her in this man's eyes. As if anything could worsen the opinion he already held, she scorned herself.

'No, perhaps not,' he conceded. 'But at a guess I'd say you haven't slept with him. That is if you're running true to form. Tris said you seemed cold, almost emotionless. He believed it was because some man had hurt you in the past. I think that was part of your at-traction for him. Tris always was an impractical dreamer, easily imposed upon. I think he saw you as a challenge and himself as some kind of knight errant who would restore your faith in men.' Keir's voice was bitingly sar-donic. 'Just what sort of woman *are* you, Venna?' Keir went on. Now he sounded genuinely curious. 'Explain yourself to me—if you can.'

'There's nothing to explain,' she said quietly, 'apart from what I've already told you. I wanted a child, I didn't want a husband. It's as simple as that.'

'Nothing is ever that simple,' he argued. 'For instance, you still haven't given me a good reason why you changed your mind.' His tone became speculative. 'I presume you do intend to marry Little. Or have you been leading him up the garden path? Were you just securing your business interests?'

'No!' Venna was stung into an unwary retort. 'My engagement to Terry was quite genuine.'

'Was?' She didn't realise she had laid any particular emphasis on the word, but he pounced on the past tense and, as she remained silent, '*Was*, Venna?'

'Oh, all right,' she told him wearily. He was bound to find out some time. 'So we had a row and I broke it off. But it might not have happened,' she accused, 'if you hadn't turned up...'

'Giving Little the idea that now he could get rid of Gemma?' He was certainly shrewd.

'Yes.'

'But it also gave you a very convenient excuse, didn't it?'

'It wasn't an excuse.' But wasn't it? Since breaking off her engagement to Terry, Venna realised, she'd scarcely spared him a thought. She certainly wasn't broken-hearted. Perhaps she had never really been in love with him. Maybe she was more like her half-sister than she'd realised. Perhaps she wasn't capable of falling really, deeply in love. It was a chilling thought.

'So you're a free agent again!' There was something vaguely disquieting in the thoughtful way he said it. And Venna's uneasy intuition was confirmed when he went on, 'Which means there's nothing to stop you falling in with my plans.'

'There's still the shop,' she improvised hurriedly. 'Breaking off my engagement doesn't necessarily affect my business partnership.'

'Doesn't it?' he asked drily. 'Don't you think you might find the atmosphere a little strained?'

She would, of course, if that had been her real intention. She realised that. She wasn't the naïve little idiot he obviously thought her. But she was still fighting total capitulation to Keir's plans for her and Gemma.

'Terry and I may well get back together again,' she said mendaciously. 'He's had time to think about it. Perhaps he didn't realise before how much Gemma meant to me. He might see things my way now. He might decided to accept Gemma, to adopt her, even.' She knew that was impossible, of course, but it fooled Keir.

'No way!' Keir said sharply. 'My brother's child isn't up for adoption. Do you think I'd stand by and see her put to that kind of risk?'

'Risk?'

'How often do you see reports of children being subjected to cruelty? Children of previous marriages, or previous relationships?'

'Terry would never go that far!' Venna said positively. Terry might not like children, nor Gemma in particular, but he wasn't a monster.

But Keir was inexorable.

'And how do you know your feelings for her might not change when other children come along?'

'I could never, never stop loving Gemma!' Venna said. Her voice shook with the intensity of her feelings. 'Whatever else you think of me, you've *got* to believe that!' She was suddenly on the brink of tears, and it must have sounded in her voice.

'All right!' he said brusquely. 'Don't get hysterical. I do believe you. In any case, you're going to have ample opportunity to prove it to me. Your broken engagement has given me the perfect solution to all our problems.'

'Why? I don't see how...'

'Obviously the only way I can protect Gemma's interests and give her her rightful name is for me to marry you.'

CHAPTER FOUR

THERE was an aghast silence in which Venna felt sure she must have somehow misheard him.

'Wh-what did you say?'

'I think you heard me well enough the first time. And I'm afraid it's your only alternative now.'

'Oh, I heard you,' she retorted, 'but I couldn't believe my ears. It's such a totally ridiculous suggestion.'

'As I said, it's the only choice you've got now. If you hadn't behaved so rashly... Anyway, it seems eminently sensible to me. You're obviously not in love with Little.'

'You can't know that,' Venna protested.

'Can't I? Women in the throes of infatuation don't usually quibble over a child's future as you've done—hence the tragic cases I mentioned earlier. If you'd been in love with Little, you'd have married him and worried about the consequences afterwards.'

He could be right, Venna thought, though she didn't think she would ever have acted in that way. But then, it seemed she had never really been in love with Terry.

'You're not in love with Little,' Keir repeated, 'and I'm certainly not expecting you to love me. So far as you and I are concerned this would be purely a matter of convenience. In effect, you'd be keeping the independence you crave so much. You can even carry on working if you like, and,' he emphasised, 'that way you'd be able to keep Gemma.'

'I didn't intend to part with her in any case,' she retorted. 'You know that!' But it was a feeble defiance. Venna was only too aware that, if Keir probed deeply enough, he would discover the truth about Gemma's

68

parentage. And if he did so he would find he had an equal, if not a better claim to the child. It didn't occur to her until much later that marriage to Keir, his legal guardianship of Gemma, would also inevitably result in discovery. 'It's a ridiculous idea!' she repeated, but with less conviction. 'Suppose, later on, you were to meet someone you really wanted to marry, what then?'

'We'll cross that bridge if we ever come to it. But at my age—I'm thirty-nine, by the way—it isn't likely. I think I've managed to pass unscathed through the dangerous years of stupid infatuations.'

'I don't believe you've never had a girlfriend,' Venna said.

'Of course I've had girlfriends,' irritably, 'but none I ever felt impelled to spend the rest of my life with. You see, Venna, I don't believe in love any more than you do.'

But she did believe in love, Venna thought sadly. She wanted to love and be loved. Without that supreme gift, the quality of life could never be the same.

'That may be so, but...' The more she thought about it, the more his suggestion disturbed her. Even for Gemma's sake she wasn't sure she could marry a man who didn't love her, who didn't want her love. If she were merely to live with Keir Trevelyan, there was still the danger she might grow to like him. She might even grow fond of him. After all, that was what happened in many arranged marriages, in other cultures. Already she was aware of his attraction, and she wasn't sure she could afford to take that risk. Another objection occurred to her.

'And what about your mother? You didn't want her to know that I'm...I'm Gemma's mother. How is she going to take it if you marry the woman she thinks is...is...?'

'Responsible for Tris's death?' He shrugged. 'She may not like it at first. But when she knows that's what it took to secure Gemma's future...' And what a further source of prejudice that would give Mrs Trevelyan, Venna thought unhappily, if she were told her only remaining son had been forced into a loveless marriage. She tried again.

'But even if I were mad enough to agree to marry you, there's still the bookshop. I...'

'Easy! Get Little to buy out your share in the business and start up again down there.'

'I do realise that's the thing to do,' she retorted sarcastically. 'I was taught the book trade by a professional. What I'm trying to say is that Terry couldn't afford to buy me out. That was why he needed a partner in the first place—insufficient capital.' She didn't add what she strongly suspected, that Terry's recent buying spree had put them both in the red at the bank.

'I'll set you up in another business.'

'No!' she retorted sharply. 'I couldn't accept money from you.'

'Not even as my wife?'

'No,' she said positively. 'Not in the kind of marriage you're suggesting.'

'I should have thought that was just the kind of marriage to incorporate a business arrangement.' Then, as she made a negative sound, 'All right,' impatiently, 'I'll find another investor to take over your side of the business.'

'Now hold on!' Venna exclaimed angrily. She jumped up, unable to stay in her chair a moment longer. This semi-darkness was frustrating. She had never liked negotiating blind. 'I'm quite capable of sorting out my own business arrangements, thank you. And just because you're Gemma's uncle doesn't give you the right to start dictating to me about what I should do with my life. I haven't said I want to sell out. I happen to like the shop we have now. I like living and working in Southport. I've got relations nearby, in Preston.'

'You said you liked Cornwall,' he reminded her.

'Yes, but I don't know anyone there. I've just begun to make friends in Southport.'

'You would have Gemma—and,' he added drily, 'me.'

'Oh, yes,' she muttered sarcastically, 'some friend! And that's another thing. You! You just calmly suggest that I should marry you, a man I've known only a few days, a man I don't...' She'd nearly said love. But she wasn't supposed to care about love. 'Why should I be the one to give up everything?'

'You're not suggesting, I hope, that I should move to Southport?'

'No, of course not. But why should I uproot myself and... Oh, damn!' In her fury she had forgotten the rearranged room and the many obstructions in her path. An unwary step brought her to the edge of one of the mattresses. She stumbled against it, was unable to regain her balance and fell, hitting her head against the arm of Keir's chair.

Through a haze of pain she heard him exclaim, heard him fumble for matches and strike one. In the light of the candle she saw his swarthy face as he bent over her.

'Of all the idiotic...' Then his voice altered. 'You've hurt yourself! Let me see.' His expression became concerned. But then, of course, he wouldn't want the additional responsibility of an injured woman on his hands. Nevertheless his fingers were gentle as he removed her trembling hands from her head and explored her brow. He swore under his breath as he discovered the already swelling disfigurement.

'I'm all right,' she snapped. The painful accident had brought her close to tears again. 'If you'll just leave me alone for a minute...' But he ignored her protest, and she was disconcerted to discover just how pleasant was the touch of his cool hand on her throbbing head.

It was their first real physical contact, and she was appalled to find herself thinking how good it would be, in times of trouble, to be able to rely on the strength of such a man as this. Even though he wasn't in love with her, she knew that if she did marry him she and Gemma would always feel safe. She'd never had that sense of security when Terry was around. She was proud of her self-reliant nature, but it would be nice, she thought wistfully, to have someone to lean on occasionally.

But it was her injury, she told herself, that was making her give in to such weak fantasies, that made her long for Keir to hold her in his arms and comfort her. She was quite certain the idea of doing so had never even crossed his mind. So far as he was concerned, she was just a clumsy nuisance.

'Leave me alone!' she almost wailed.

Despite her renewed protests, he helped her to her feet and made her sit down again. He insisted on making a cold compress from a damp tea-towel, and applied it himself to her brow.

'At least the skin isn't broken,' he reassured her. 'But there'll be an unsightly bruise for a few days. And I reckon very shortly you're going to have a humdinger of a headache. You'd better get into bed, and I'll bring you a hot drink and a couple of aspirins.' As she rose unsteadily he steered her towards the corner where Gemma was already fast asleep, undisturbed by their murmured conversation. 'Do you need any help?'

'No, thank you!' She was relieved when he took her at her word and headed for the kitchen once more. The idea of him helping her to undress made her quiver inside. She must be going down with a cold or something, Venna decided as she scrambled out of her clothes. She'd been experiencing some very odd sensations the last couple of days that could only be put down to the onset of some malaise. And now, as Keir had predicted, her head was aching violently.

The hot drink and the aspirin did their job, for she fell asleep surprisingly quickly.

She woke again in the middle of the night, and for a moment she couldn't think where she was or what had disturbed her. Then she remembered everything, and in the same instant saw Keir Trevelyan's large frame silhouetted against the firelight. It was the sound of a log rolling into the grate that had roused her. She sat up, then could not repress a groan as the movement set her head throbbing again.

'Did I wake you?' Keir asked. 'Sorry about that. How's the head?' Deftly he avoided the obstacles in his path and came to crouch beside her. She felt his breath warm on her cheek and lay back hastily.

'Painful,' she admitted. Then, as she registered the fact that he was still dressed, 'Haven't you been to bed yet? What time is it?'

'Two o'clock. I may have dozed off once or twice in the chair. But I felt someone ought to keep an eye on the fire. We can't be a hundred per cent certain that chimney's OK.'

'Oh, goodness!' Venna exclaimed penitently. 'I ought to be taking a turn at that. Look, you get some rest. I'll watch the fire. I'm sure I shan't sleep another wink. I'm wide awake now.'

'So am I. How would it be if I made us both a hot drink? The kettle has boiled once. Then we'll talk if you like.'

'What about?' she asked suspiciously, and felt rather than saw his shrug.

'Me, you, what makes us both tick.' He abandoned his crouching position and sat on the edge of her mattress. 'I'm particularly interested in what's made you the way you are.'

'Why?' she asked. Furtively she shifted her position. The semi-darkness, the bedding, gave their situation an uneasy hint of intimacy. He was too close for comfort.

'Because,' impatiently, 'it has a bearing on any decision we make about Gemma's future.'

'Oh!' She thought about it for a moment, then, 'All right.' Once again she had to put herself in Shelagh's shoes, speak with her voice. 'I suppose,' she began, 'it was mainly our upbringing.'

'Our?' God, but he was quick. He'd given evidence of that before. She must be more careful.

'*My* upbringing,' she amended hastily, but he was not diverted.

'You said our!'

'I had a sister,' Venna admitted reluctantly. 'Or rather a half-sister.'

'*Had?*'

'She's dead. Anyway,' edgily, 'we're not talking about her.' If only he knew! Briefly but succinctly Venna outlined her childhood and adolescence, her mother's betrayal by two husbands, Granny Birtles' less than subtle indoctrination of her grandchildren. 'Anyway, it made us—me—wary of getting involved in any relationships. It seemed better not to risk being hurt, to be independent of men.'

'And what about your half-sister? Did she feel the same way?'

'I . . . Yes,' Venna said flatly. Since she was playing the part of Shelagh, there was no point in revealing that their opinions had been totally opposed.

'So it's emotional relationships you're afraid of. Not *physical* ones, obviously,' he said with a dry emphasis that made Venna flush. 'That ties in with the side of yourself you showed to Tris. But it doesn't altogether tie in with *my* observations of you.'

'Oh! What do you mean?' Venna asked nervously.

'In all our dealings so far, I've found you highly emotional.'

'Only where Gemma is concerned.'

'Exactly. That's the whole basis of my argument. You're not prepared to risk loving any man. Obviously your engagement to Little was a matter of expediency.'

She didn't bother to contradict him. As Shelagh, she wouldn't anyway. 'But doesn't your love for the child make you just as vulnerable? She'll grow up, grow away from you, or,' significantly, 'you could lose her.'

'Not to you,' Venna said with spirit, though inwardly she was quaking. 'If that's what you're trying to imply.'

'Strangely enough, I wasn't. There are other losses, through accident or sickness and death. No love is risk-free.' He was preaching to the converted if he did but know it, and Venna had no ready answer for him this time. 'It can't have been easy, bringing Gemma up on your own. No one to share the responsibilities, the worries?'

'There haven't been any worries,' Venna could say truthfully. 'Gemma's always been a healthy little girl.' But she crossed her fingers as she spoke. To say it aloud seemed to be tempting fate.

'How did you manage when she was tiny? It must have been difficult for a working mother.'

She hadn't *had* to look after Gemma when she was first born.

'I managed,' Venna said evasively.

'Did you breast-feed her?'

Venna shifted uneasily. She felt her cheeks going hot. She was unsure whether his interest was academic or mildly prurient.

'No,' she said shortly, for as a working mother Shelagh hadn't been able to breast-feed Gemma. 'Now, could we discuss something else? Talking about myself isn't something I enjoy.'

'Really?' He sounded astonished. 'For a lot of women it's their favourite form of indulgence.'

'Well, it isn't mine. Didn't you mention something about wanting a hot drink? Shall I make it?' She made a move to scramble up, but a large hand restrained her.

'No, I'll go. It won't take a minute to bring the kettle back to the boil. You keep warm. You know,' he said consideringly as he straightened his long body, 'you're a constant source of surprise to me.'

'In what way?' Venna asked cautiously. It didn't sound like a compliment, and she was quivering oddly since that moment when he had gripped her arm. It hadn't been a painful contact, just unnerving.

'I didn't expect to like you,' he said over his shoulder as he moved into the adjoining kitchen.

She hadn't expected to like him either, she thought. But, despite the threat he posed to her possession of Gemma, she couldn't dislike him. In fact, under different circumstances... But she refused to consider that.

'And now?' she asked when she could bear the silence no longer.

'Now,' he drawled, 'I have to admit you have some redeeming features.' Why, the condescending...!

'Thank you, kind sir!' Venna said with explosive sarcasm. But with her innate sense of honesty she knew she couldn't blame him for his confusion. He wasn't dealing with the woman he had expected to meet. No wonder he was finding inconsistencies.

'But I suppose the redeeming features are what ensnared my brother,' he went on as if she hadn't spoken. 'I'm not my brother, Venna,' he said as he re-entered the room, carrying two mugs. 'Never forget that. Don't think you can pull the wool over my eyes. You've tried once and failed.'

For a moment her temper flared dangerously, then with enormous self-control she decided to ignore the taunt.

'Venna!' He repeated her name musingly. 'Short for Morvenna, of course. It was the abbreviation that caused some of the difficulty I had in tracing you. It's a Cornish name.' It was a statement, but there was a question implied too.

'My father was Cornish. Morvenna was his idea, but I prefer to be called Venna.'

'The abbreviation suits you,' Keir commented. 'It has a quality of uniqueness. As I'm beginning to believe you do. And did your sister have a Cornish name, too?'

'No, she was called Shelagh,' Venna said shortly. She didn't spell it for him and she didn't want to talk about her half-sister. 'I thought we were going to stop discussing me,' she said as she took the proffered drink. 'How about a bit of fair exchange?'

'All right,' he agreed. 'What do you want to know?'

Venna wasn't quite sure. She sought for a safe topic.

'What do you do—for a living, I mean?' Inwardly she apologised to the bristling spectre of Granny Birtles who had brought the half-sisters up to believe such questions were impolite. Just as you never asked anyone what they earned or how much they had paid for an item.

'I run the family firm. My grandfather founded it. My father took over until his death, then my brother and I were partners. Now it's solely my responsibility.'

'What sort of firm?' she asked when there seemed to be a danger of another silence.

'Tris didn't tell you that, either?'

'Er—no. At least, I don't remember anything...'

'We deal in property...'

'Oh, an estate agent.' It was a relief to find he was in such an ordinary profession. Somehow he gave quite the opposite impression.

'Er...yes.' He sounded mildly amused, but she couldn't think why. 'So I'd have no difficulty, would I, in finding you suitable premises down in Cornwall, to start another bookshop.'

This broad hint probably explained the amusement, but she ignored the suggestion. Still, at least it gave her a subject for her next question.

'You live in Cornwall, too? With your mother?'

'Only at weekends. I also have a flat in London. Anything else you'd like to know?' There was a mocking note in his voice which incensed Venna. After all, he'd made her give chapter and verse about herself.

'There's a lot I *need* to know about you,' she retorted. 'But I don't think you're the best person for me to ask. You're bound to be prejudiced.'

'I suppose you want a character reference.' Again she suspected he was laughing at her.

'I most certainly do!' she told him emphatically. 'How do I know you're any more fit to be Gemma's guardian than you think I am? You've told me you're not married. What do you know about bringing up a small child?'

'Very little,' he surprised her by admitting. 'Which is why you and I have to come to some agreement. You hadn't forgotten that we have some unfinished business to discuss? I was perfectly serious when I suggested that you marry me and that we share Gemma. It seems a fair enough arrangement to me. So, how about it, Venna?'

'You can't expect me to decide something so important just like that.' Instead of totally rejecting his suggestion, Venna found herself almost pleading with him. She felt strangely weak and vulnerable, almost inclined to agree without further argument. It was that time of night, of course, the small hours after midnight when the human spirit and body were at their lowest ebb.

'Not at this instant, perhaps. But obviously you haven't entirely discounted the idea.' His perception disconcerted her. 'And we do have to get things straightened out as soon as possible,' he insisted. 'Once the thaw sets in and we get out of here, I don't want to waste any more time. Before then, I want your decision one way or another.'

Over the next day or two Venna found herself anxiously watching the weather, which seemed to her to have taken on the role of arbiter of her fate. For with a change in the temperature it seemed her whole way of life must alter. She'd decided, though she hadn't told Keir yet, that she was going to agree to the lesser of two evils, that her role in Cornwall should be that of Gemma's nanny. She hadn't actually admitted any reason to herself, but for the sake of her own peace of mind she knew she dared not accept the alternative.

But in her heart of hearts Venna knew she had to do whatever it took to keep Gemma. And being married to Keir Trevelyan might not have been so bad, she caught herself thinking rather wistfully. He was very much the dominant male, of course. But there was strength and reassurance in his dominance.

He could be kind, she had discovered. He'd been concerned and gentle when she had injured herself. He liked children. In the past day or two he and Gemma had become fast friends, and Venna had a great deal of confidence in her small niece's reactions to adults.

Because they were so confined, Keir had taken the trouble to clear a large area outside the cottage door. Here, well wrapped up and supervised by one or other of them, Gemma could play. One morning he built a snowman for the child, and taught her how to make snowballs and use the snowman for target practice.

Venna was busy in the kitchen, baking, but the deep, pleasant sound of male laughter and her niece's higher-pitched, delighted chuckles brought her to the door to see what was going on. She hardly recognised the normally grave-faced Keir in the man whose mirth-filled face turned towards her.

She looked at him with slowly growing recognition. She'd often wondered what it would be like. So this was how it happened! It wasn't as novelists would have you believe, a sudden bolt from the blue. It was just this quiet knowledge, this acceptance of the inevitable that had been growing on her for several days. She had fallen in love with Keir Trevelyan.

She responded to his smile with her own reciprocal sparkle. For the moment, all was joyful understanding. Fear hadn't yet entered into her realisation. Urged by Gemma, she joined in the fun.

She wasn't quite sure afterwards who had started it—and it had only been to amuse Gemma, she assured herself—but suddenly she and Keir were snowballing each other. For a short while all her inhibitions in his company fled, and she was as exhilarated as the child. It was almost possible, she thought, to imagine they were a family enjoying each other's company.

She soon realised that Keir's aim was far more accurate than hers. But she also noted that he took care not to inflict any injury. One of her shots, however, more random than the rest, caught him on one swarthy cheek.

'Oh! I'm sorry,' she giggled breathlessly. 'I didn't mean to...' She broke off as she saw the expression on his face. Not one of annoyance, but of rueful amusement, for Gemma was chuckling wildly and the child's laughter was infectious. Venna herself began to laugh. It was a warm, delightful sound, the man thought, surprisingly deep for her slight frame.

'Right!' Keir warned in mock indignation. 'Laugh at me, would you, you two? OK, you've asked for it.' He swooped upon Gemma, lifted her and twirled her around his head, which only served to increase the child's mirth.

Smiling, somewhat fatuously, she realised, at her niece's enjoyment, Venna did not understand at first that she had been included in Keir's threat. She gave a little shriek of protest as he grabbed her. He held her aloft as he had held the child, and Venna marvelled at the strength in those muscular arms and shoulders that could lift her above his head so effortlessly.

He held her threateningly over a drift of snow, and Venna was wondering uncertainly whether he would actually execute the threat when he set her back on her feet. As he did so he lost his footing on the well-trampled of her bra, he softly enquired, 'All right with you, Whitney?'

Too full to speak, she nodded, and she knew her reply had been received when, her fastenings undone, she felt his hands at the naked skin at her back. When that same warm, gentle touch caressed round to her front and he held each swollen globe of her breasts in his hands, Whitney knew that she had consented to anything he asked of her.

'Oh, Sloan!' she cried in delight and anguish of wanting when his fingers tormented the hardened peaks he had created.

'I want you, sweet Whitney,' Sloan breathed. 'Is it the same with you?'

'You know it is,' she said huskily, and gave him her lips, feeling only the first pangs of shyness when he went to remove her top. 'C-can we have the light out?' she asked, and it seemed that, even if Sloan was not aware of the reason for her request, he was ready to grant her anything. Because, leaving her for only a moment, he plunged the room into darkness.

When he came back to her, he was without his shirt, and Whitney gloried in the freedom he allowed her as her hands roved over his broad shoulders and she ca- ressed her way round to the front of his chest.

Then, with the minimum amount of fuss, 'Put your arms up, sweet love,' Sloan instructed her, and in a few seconds her top had been disposed of, her bra along with it, and Sloan's hair-roughened chest was against her silken skin.

Again she wanted to cry his name, and might well have done, but suddenly his lips were claiming hers, and his kiss was deepening, and Whitney knew then, as her need for him soared to match his desire for her, that there would be no turning back.

In the darkness they stood together, and in that darkness Sloan undid her skirt. Whitney stepped out of it when it slid to the ground, and she clutched on to Sloan as he removed the rest of her clothes.

Almost carried by him as, caressing her, kissing her, he moved to the bed and divested himself of his clothing, Whitney knew only that she was in love with Sloan and that this was right for her.

'Sweet Whitney,' he breathed, and, as his mouth came over hers, he moved with her on to the bed and pulled down the covers.

In an enchanted world, she knew nothing but the de-light of the touch of the man she loved as he trailed kisses down her throat to finally capture her breasts. 'Sloan!' she cried as his fingers did magical things to her spine. And, 'Sloan!' she cried again when her need was more than she could bear.

She was ready to beg him to take her when he at last moved his body to her. But her cry of pleasure was sud-denly diminished at the first shaft of pain. This time she did not have to call his name or say anything. For Sloan immediately knew what her cry of pain had been about. What her shy wish to have the light out was all about. She knew it the instant his body stilled.

'Oh, my G...!' he exclaimed in an awed kind of voice. 'Oh, my dear—you're a virgin!'

But Whitney, her desire for him greater than her pain, was suddenly in dreadful fear that Sloan might not want her.

'Please,' she implored him. 'You can't leave me like this. I want you, I need you.' Ready to beg, she clung to him.

'Oh, my love,' Sloan cried, and as Whitney gripped him and held him close to her naked body in panic that he might go from her, 'Oh, my very dear Whitney,' he breathed hoarsely, and gently, his touch so considerate that it was almost ethereal, he tenderly made her his.

CHAPTER EIGHT

DAWN had tiptoed through the night sky when Whitney stirred in her sleep. On any other Sunday, she might have turned over and slumbered on, but for some reason she felt compelled, this Sunday morning, to open her eyes. Pink colour washed her creamy cheeks as her waking green eyes fastened on the bare masculine chest which was only inches away from her gaze. A warm, dreamy smile picked up the corners of her mouth, and her eyes travelled upwards until she met, full on, the grey eyes of the man who was propped up on one elbow and who had been observing her while she slept.

She did not feel shocked to see him there; only, as memory raced in of how they had lain naked with each other and were still naked, a little shy.

But her shyness appeared to delight Sloan, for as she looked at him, a tender smile appeared on his mouth and in his eyes. 'Hello, my love,' he whispered, and it was then that Whitney, with an overflowing heart, knew that Sloan loved her.

'Hello,' she whispered back huskily, and she began to tingle anew when, beneath the covers, his arm came around her waist and he pulled her naked body towards him and kissed her.

With his mouth gently teasing her lips apart with tender kisses, Whitney was soon more glorying in their nakedness with each other than overwhelmingly con-scious of it.

'Oh, Sloan,' she cried shakily, and she knew more rapture as his hands caressed her body and he brought her to the peak of desire.

'Am I allowed to look at you now?' he asked tenderly, reminding her of the way she had wanted the light out last night.

Unable to tell him yes or no, Whitney's answer was in the way she gave him her lips in utter supplication. Gently, unhurriedly, Sloan uncovered her, and gently he kissed her belly, her breasts, and her mouth.

'You're more than beautiful,' he told her, and as he kissed her again, and as their bodies touched, he looked tenderly into her eyes and promised, 'Sweet love, it will be better for you this time.'

It was still early when Whitney awoke for the second time that morning, but when she opened her eyes there was no Sloan propped up on one elbow looking down at her. Nor was his head on the pillow beside her.

Then she heard a sound somewhere in the house, and she realised that perhaps the sound of Sloan moving around downstairs was what had awakened her a few moments ago.

For some minutes she lay there just glorying in the way she and Sloan had been with each other. Never had she imagined that she would know such total freedom with him. To touch him, his body, as he touched her.

Whitney supposed that she should be feeling a little shocked that, when she'd had no plans to spend the night away from her flat, she should not only do that, but should spend the night in bed with Sloan. But, loving him with all her being, she did not feel shocked. More, she felt warmed through and through and sublimely elated, for the simple reason that as she loved Sloan, so Sloan loved her.

Of course, he hadn't said that he loved her. Not in so many words he hadn't. But, as Whitney left the bed to go to the adjoining bathroom to turn on the shower, she knew that love her he did. She had only to remember the way they had made love at dawn to know that. For the way he had made love to her that second time was, in contrast to the first, as thrilling as it was staggering. Only then had she realised how, for her untutored sake, he had kept a rein on his passion the first time. His thought then had been more for her than for his own needs, she was sure of it. Which had to mean that he loved her, didn't it?

Realising that doubts were starting to edge in about something over which she had been pretty near certain only a short while ago, Whitney showered hurriedly. She needed to see Sloan again. She needed to have that re-assurance that it was as she believed, that he did love her.

Feeling that she would only have to see his face to have the truth of her thoughts endorsed, Whitney quickly dried, and she was soon dressed, save for the primrose and white top which had come to grief while she had been washing up last night. She had the top in her grip when, on the floor by the foot of the bed, she espied the shirt which Sloan had been about to hand her when he had instead gathered her into his arms.

She wasn't even thinking when she dropped the garment in her hands down on to the bed, and got into Sloan's over-large shirt instead. Rolling up the sleeves as she went, she left the bedroom in some haste, wanting to see him, and went swiftly down the stairs.

As she reached the hall, a sound in the drawing-room attracted her attention and, as a stray trace of shyness suddenly made itself felt, she slowed her pace. But, as she approached the drawing-room, she saw that the door was open, and her need to see Sloan suddenly became greater than her shyness. She had stepped inside the room when she stopped stone-dead. For the person there was not Sloan but, busy with a duster, his housekeeper. And Whitney, who had never in her life before left any man's bed to be confronted by a housekeeper, did not know how to handle it. Especially when the look on the house-keeper's face made it plain that, though it wouldn't take her long to guess that she had shared her master's bed, she had not until just then so much as known that she was in the house.

'Good morning, Mrs Orton,' she tried to cheerfully brazen it out.

'Good morning,' Mrs Orton mumbled in reply, but she had nothing else to add, and Whitney felt more uncomfortable than ever. Suddenly she was overpowered by the knowledge that she had on Sloan's shirt, and any ability she had to brazen the situation out promptly deserted her.

Wishing that Sloan, with his easy sophistication, would come and extract her from this uncomfortable moment, Whitney, growing a shade more uncertain that Sloan did in fact love her, found that she was looking for excuses for why she had stayed overnight.

'I—er—expected Mrs Illingworth to be here,' she volunteered. And when the housekeeper looked at her blankly, and gave every impression of seeming not to have the first idea of why she should have expected her employer's mother to be at Heathlands, Whitney suddenly caught on. 'Oh, it's all right, Mrs Orton,' she smiled. 'I know all about Mrs Illingworth being—a little—confused.'

'Confused?' Mrs Orton repeated, and while Whitney was thinking what a loyal person she was, the house-keeper went on to give Whitney her first inkling that something was wrong. 'If you're referring to Mr Illingworth's mother, she's Mrs Eastwood now,' she stated, and while Whitney was taking in the news that Sloan's mother had remarried at some time, she was adding, 'But I don't know where you got the idea from that she's confused, I'm sure I don't. I spoke to her myself when she telephoned Mr Illingworth yesterday, and although we didn't talk for very long before I went to find him for her, she was as bright and alert as she ever was.'

'Oh—I see,' Whitney said slowly, trying to get over her surprise at what the housekeeper had just said by being glad that, by the sound of it, Sloan's mother was making rapid strides back to full health. 'Well, I'm glad that Mrs Illing ... Mrs Eastwood,' she corrected herself, 'is so much better after her accident. I ...'

'Mrs Eastwood hasn't been in any accident!' Mrs Orton informed her, and seemed astonished that Whitney should think she had.

Shaken rigid, Whitney refused to listen to what her intelligence was trying to tell her. 'But when she phoned yesterday, she must have rung you from the hospital,' she insisted brightly.

'Hospital?' Mrs Orton exclaimed, astounded. But Whitney was the more astounded of the two, though utterly stunned was a more accurate description of how she felt when the housekeeper told her, 'Mr Illingworth's mother didn't ring from any hospital, she rang from her home in America.'

'America!' Whitney echoed stupidly, one part of her brain just refusing to function and accept what the housekeeper was telling her.

'Mrs Eastwood's husband is an American, so they decided to live there,' Mrs Orton said, as if that explained everything.

As some receptive part of Whitney's brain began to acknowledge that Sloan must have lied, lied, and lied to her, her heart started to fracture. By some great good fortune, though, her plentiful supply of pride began to stir. And as she started to hurt with a pain such as she had never known, Whitney was aware that only she was going to know it. Even as Mrs Orton stood there, having answered her questions only because, clearly, she wanted to get on and tidy up the drawing-room but was too polite to dust while her employer's guest was addressing her, Whitney was biting down the pain.

Spotting her brown shoulder-bag down by the couch, she masked her hurt by going over and bending down to pick it up. 'I must have got it wrong about Mrs Eastwood's accident,' she said over her shoulder.

'Must have,' Mrs Orton agreed, and went on as Whitney delayed in straightening up, 'I've only become acquainted with her in the year I've worked for Mr Illingworth, but I've never heard of Mrs Eastwood having a day's illness—and,' she added as Whitney straightened, 'she wouldn't have phoned to say that she and her husband had made up their minds on the spur of the moment to take a cruise, and would be away two months, if there was anything the matter with either of them.'

'She certainly wouldn't,' Whitney agreed, but she was aware that, though outwardly calm and composed, she was breaking up inside. Pride alone was responsible for the smile she showed the housekeeper as she told her, 'I must be on my way.' But, along with pride, rage was starting to nip, and latent murderous traits were beginning to make themselves felt. 'Do you know where Sloan is?' she asked pleasantly.

'The doors of the particular garage he uses were open and his car was gone when my son-in-law dropped me off on his way fishing,' Mrs Orton replied.

'Oh, he's probably out somewhere, then,' Whitney said, only by pure grit managing to keep her smile in place as it hit her that, by his very cavalier attitude, Sloan was making it seem as though she was nothing more than—than a—one-night stand! Appalled that that was about all she was to him, Whitney's rage was momentarily buried and she knew only that she had to get out of there, and fast. 'It was nice meeting you again,' she murmured, though as she went from the room Whitney doubted that the housekeeper would remember her from their previous meeting. She hoped, with all she had, that she would forget this meeting too.

Whitney was in the hall and was about to leave Heathlands when, at the solid front door, her swamped feelings began to revive. She was already starting to feel angry again, when, in the act of hitching her shoulder-bag further over her shoulder and simultaneously stretching out a hand to the door, she became aware that she was still wearing Sloan's shirt.

And suddenly, she was infuriated. As she recalled how she had lovingly wrapped the shirt around her when she had put it on, Whitney's rage went into overdrive and was almost past enduring.

Without any memory of how she had climbed the stairs and came to be on the first-floor landing, Whitney went storming into Sloan's bedroom, her shaking fingers already tearing at the buttons of the shirt. It was imposs- ible for her to keep her eyes averted from the over-large bed, and she hurled Sloan's shirt from her.

Sparks were shooting from her eyes as she claimed her primrose and white top and, without regard to its damp and creased condition, put it on.

snow. Instead of Venna being dropped into the snow-drift, they both collapsed into it, Keir's weight on top of her, making them sink several inches through the crusted layer.

Winded, Venna could not move immediately, and when she tried she found she was trapped. With her breath regained she looked up at Keir to make some humorous protest. The words and the amusement died on her lips at the sight of his suddenly arrested expression.

He had made no attempt to move. His body still half covered hers, and his face was only inches away. Grey eyes that were usually steely in their intensity looked into her, and something seemed to kindle in their depths, thawing them to a warmer hue.

'Did you know,' he said huskily, 'that you have flour on your nose?'

Her gaze shifted to his mouth, to the full, sensual lower lip, and she found herself wondering what it would be like if he kissed her, wishing that he would. So strong was the feeling that she almost believed he was about to do so.

Sensation twisted violently within her, a pang of something urgent, primitive, almost frightening in its intensity.

For a long instant grey eyes held green. Then, with a sudden lithe movement, Keir was on his feet and pulling her up.

'Sorry about that!' He sounded a little breathless, considering he too had had time to recover. 'I didn't intend anything like that to happen.' The words were straightforward enough. But somehow, from his tone of voice, Venna received the impression that he wasn't referring only to their fall. Then she decided she must be mistaken as, more matter-of-factly, he consulted his watch, then said briskly, 'Time for lunch and some of those pastries you've been baking.'

'Oh, lord!' Venna clapped a hand to her mouth. 'I hope they aren't burnt.' Such mundane things as cooking had been furthest from her mind for the last ten minutes.

After lunch each day, Gemma usually had a nap. Despite the change in their circumstances and surroundings, Venna had tried to keep her niece to her normal routine. An amenable child, Gemma had accepted the situation.

'Have you noticed a slight change in the weather?' Keir asked as, with Gemma settled, Venna returned to the kitchen, a little shy of being alone with Keir now that she had recognised her feelings for him. He was washing up the lunch things. From the very first day of his arrival he had insisted on sharing in the chores. 'Don't you think it seems a little milder?'

Venna *had* felt warmer, but had put it down to exertion. Now she wondered. Was this the beginning of the thaw? If so, it meant their sojourn here was over. Her heart sank. Just as their isolation here had seemed about to become an idyll, it looked like being over.

'If I'm right,' Keir went on, not looking at her, and thus not seeing her dismayed expression, 'another twenty-four hours could see us on our way out of here. Better start making up your mind, Venna.'

CHAPTER FIVE

'I HAVE made up my mind,' she told him quietly as she picked up a tea-towel and began to dry the dishes he'd washed. That moment when she had recognised her love for him had consolidated the decision she'd already made.

'Oh?' She could feel his penetrating gaze on her down-bent face.

'Yes.' She kept her eyes averted from his, deliberately intent on her task, rubbing the plate she held as though determined to erase the floral pattern. She felt her face colour as she said, 'I've decided to go along with your first suggestion.'

He made no immediate answer, and at last, puzzled by his silence, she had to look up. He was leaning back against the sink, arms folded, regarding her steadily. It was impossible to gauge his reaction from his expression.

'You mean, despite what you said before, you're now willing to pose as Gemma's nanny?' He looked and sounded puzzled.

'Yes. But only to spare your mother's feelings,' she told him quickly. It was true, but it wasn't her only motive. 'At least until she gets to know me better,' she added quickly. 'I'm not giving up my rights to Gemma. Eventually you'll have to tell Mrs Trevelyan the truth. I insist on that.'

'So you think when my mother gets to know you better, *she'll* be able to forgive you?' Keir asked. There was an odd note in his voice that Venna did not understand, unless it meant that *he* never would forgive her.

She spread out her small hands in a strangely appealing gesture.

'You know your mother. I don't. I can only hope so.'

'Do you *want* forgiveness, Venna? From my mother?' He paused, then, 'From me?'

How to answer him honestly without revealing the truth, or her newly discovered feelings for him?

'I'd like to think,' she said slowly, 'that eventually Gemma's grandmother and her uncle could both understand and forgive Gemma's mother.' It was a strange, necessarily ambiguous way of putting it, but Keir didn't comment.

Instead he said, 'My second suggestion still stands, you know.' Then, impatiently, as she made no answer, 'I mean, that you should marry me.'

'I know what you meant. But,' firmly, 'I can't do that.'

'Not even for Gemma's sake?' he asked. There was a note in his voice that could almost have been pique, if she hadn't known better. She met his gaze frankly.

'If you were to insist—if it were the only way I could keep Gemma, I suppose I would marry you. But it isn't the only way, is it? I think I know enough about you to know you wouldn't be that unscrupulous.' It was a shot in the dark, an attempt at cajolery by flattery. She *didn't* know him that well. But for some reason her reply seemed to please him. Perhaps he was relieved by her refusal to marry him. 'I'm ready to acknowledge your family's right to a share in Gemma,' she went on. 'And her name can be changed by deed poll, if that's what you want.'

'Again you surprise me.' There was a warmth in his deep voice that she hadn't heard before. 'I confess, I didn't expect you to be so reasonable.'

Because he had seemed so much friendlier today, Venna was emboldened to ask him a question. It was something she'd been wondering about off and on, ever since that day when Keir had walked into the shop.

'How *did* you eventually find me? She...I didn't tell your brother where I lived.'

'No,' he said wryly, 'there wasn't much to go on. Just the name—Venna—no surname, and the fact that you ran a bookshop. At first Tris searched the length and breadth of Cornwall. You seemed to know the county so well, he believed you lived there.'

'Well, I did, as a child,' Venna confirmed.

'When that failed, he began to put together other small pieces of information you'd accidentally let slip, the odd remark about Preston and a Granny Birtles.'

Oh, Shelagh, Venna thought, and you prided yourself on having been so clever.

'Unfortunately Tris was killed before he could follow up these snippets, and that's where I came into the story.'

'But you said you used a private investigator?'

A detective on her trail! That was a bit drastic. Keir Trevelyan must have been obsessed with the idea of finding her. She shivered a little.

'With a business to run and my partner dead,' he said drily, 'I could hardly afford the time to go careering about the countryside myself. If Tris hadn't been so impulsive and he'd employed my methods, he might still have been alive today.'

'Even so, it took your detective quite a while to find me.'

'Hardly surprising since you didn't intend to be found,' was Keir's comment. 'He discovered there were quite a few Birtles in and around Preston, and by the time he found what appeared to be the right one, Granny Birtles was deceased. So then he had to see if there were any next of kin. He discovered three sisters. But when he did find them they were tough nuts to crack!'

Venna couldn't repress a chuckle.

'My eccentric great-aunts!'

'You can say that again! Apparently two of them did just about everything except bite his ankles. The third was more amenable. Aurora Freer.'

'You've got a good memory.'

'Oh, believe me, Venna, the details of this search are engraved on my memory. Anyway, Miss Freer was most voluble. She kindly supplied your correct name—Morvenna Leigh—and your address. After that, it wasn't difficult to find the right Southport bookshop.'

'And why was your brother so insistent that you find me, even when he...?' She stumbled over the words. 'Or didn't he know he was...?' At the expression on his face, her voice faded.

'That he was dying?' As Keir's face hardened, closed against her, Venna wished she hadn't asked. 'Yes, he knew. He didn't want me to avenge him, if that's what you're wondering.'

Her face paled, accentuating the green depths of her eyes and the little freckles that spangled her small nose. Tristram might not have wanted that, but how about Keir?

'Perhaps my brother was an incurable romantic, but even after your treatment of him, he still couldn't believe you were as cold, as unemotional, as you pretended to be. He made me promise to find you, to satisfy myself that you *were* as self-reliant as you made out. He had the misguided idea that you were acting out of pride, that you needed help of some kind. There was also a possibility, he told me, that his impulsive relationship with you had resulted in a pregnancy.'

'And you kept your promise,' Venna said wonderingly, 'even though you thought he was wrong about the kind of person I was.'

'Yes. I always keep my promises. Even,' he added somewhat obscurely, 'those I make to myself.' Then, 'Don't you want to know what I think now, Venna?'

She did, desperately. 'I suspect you're going to tell me anyway,' she merely said, with an attempt at dry humour, and she saw his face crease into an unwilling smile.

'Well, I certainly don't find you unemotional. Quite the contrary. In the few days I've known you I've seen you run just about the whole gamut, from anger—with me—to tenderness for your child. I'm no expert in these things, of course. But apart from what you've told me about your mother's experiences and your grandmother's prejudices, I see no reason for you to be so averse to marriage. It's true you have a fiery, independent streak, but you're no feminist.' His voice altered subtly. 'On the other hand, I do find you very *feminine*. I'll even go so far as to say I find you physically attractive. Is it perhaps that you're frigid, Venna?'

His remark about finding her physically attractive had so disconcerted her that for a moment she found it difficult to speak. Then she managed to croak, 'I-If I were, I'd scarcely have been planning to marry Terry, would I?' He didn't look convinced, and because her voice was husky she had to clear it before adding, 'And I did genuinely intend to marry him, before you can cast doubt on that again.'

'Tell me, are you very unhappy about your broken engagement?'

In a minute he would be convincing her he was really concerned about her feelings. She could imagine the ironic humour he would find in the fact that she had fallen in love with him. That was something he couldn't be allowed to discover.

'Are you unhappy?' he repeated.

There was so much subterfuge on her part that it was good to be able to tell the plain, unvarnished truth.

'No. I'm sorry things didn't work out, and I'm sorry it's going to mean the end of my working partnership with Terry, too. But I'm not unhappy.'

But with the truth her personality and that of Shelagh had become even more inextricably entangled.

'So really it does come back to your old hang-up,' Keir said. 'You thought you'd changed, but subconsciously you still didn't really want to get married. Basically, you still don't trust men. Tris was right. You *do* need help.'

He made it sound as if she needed a psychiatrist. Indignantly she told him so.

'I wouldn't go so far as to say that. The kind of help I had in mind was a relationship with a man who could teach you that not all men are untrustworthy. Tris would never have let you down, you know,' he added sadly. 'It's a pity you didn't let him prove himself.'

And what about Keir Trevelyan? He'd had women friends, but he hadn't married any of them. They must have felt let down.

But she was beginning to think like Shelagh now. She mustn't let pretence colour her own views. She realised Keir was still speaking.

'As to your business partnership with Little, I suspect it's the involvement with books that you'll miss more than anything.'

'Yes.' Venna had long since decided she must have been born with the love of books in her blood, a fascination with the beautiful bindings, a desire for the romance and knowledge within them. Her catholic taste in reading had given her a wide general knowledge, but where was the romance she longed for? she wondered wistfully.

'There I think I may be able to help, initially at any rate. I know of...someone who has a vast library in need of cataloguing. Would you be willing to undertake it?'

'I can't think of anything I'd enjoy more. But where?'

'In Cornwall, naturally.'

'How long would it take?'

'You'll be the best judge of that, when you see what's involved. Certainly until you know what your future plans are.'

Her future plans! Venna thought that night as she lay unpleasantly wide awake. And she couldn't blame her wakefulness on the somewhat lumpy mattress. Only a few short weeks ago she'd been entirely certain of the direction her life was to take. Marriage, combined with her career, caring for Gemma, her own children in due course.

Now she was certain of nothing except that she'd done the most stupid thing possible in the circumstances. She'd fallen in love with a man who believed her to be somebody and something she was not. And to tell him the truth would only make matters worse.

She must have dozed off eventually, because she was aware of being woken from time to time by the movements of an unusually restless Gemma. She hoped the child wasn't developing a cold.

It was only just beginning to get light when Venna became aware of a sound she could not at first identify. Then she slid out of her sleeping-bag and went to the window. She parted the curtains to reveal a steady 'drip, drip' of melting snow coming from the eaves above. The sun was shining and the surrounding trees, too, were losing their icy burden. The thaw Keir had predicted had begun.

All the uncertainties of the night rushed in upon her again. At the cottage there were problems enough, but once they left here those problems would multiply.

'You're up early. Everything all right?' The sound of Keir's deep voice made her start. He looked far less formidable first thing in the morning, she thought, with the dark but greying hair rumpled, his strong jawline subtly softened by a night's growth of stubble. She wished she could follow the impulse she felt, to put her arms about him and hug his head to her breast. She could just imagine his reaction if she did! Confusion made her stammer.

'D-did I wake you? I'm sorry. It's thawing.'

'Good.' He scrambled up and came to join her at the window, standing close in order to peer over her shoulder. 'It looks as if that sun might stick around and finish the job.' His large body still had the warmth of sleep and that warmth reached her, seemed to enfold her in its aura. Sensuous reaction made her shiver. 'But you're cold,' he exclaimed. 'Get dressed and we'll go out and take a look.'

She was thankful when, as he had done on every other occasion, he took his clothes into the kitchen, leaving her the privacy to scramble into her jeans and sweater. Thank God he was every inch the gentleman in such matters! She'd been very fortunate. She might have been cooped up here with an unscrupulous rogue. She pulled on an anorak, then went to join him. He was already outside.

'If this keeps on, by this afternoon I think we might risk the track. We'll assume that's the case and get everything packed into the Land Rover.'

'We've got a lot of stuff. Some of it will have to go in my car.'

'No.' He shook his head. 'Your car will have to stay here temporarily.'

'I can't just leave my car,' she began.

'You're not driving. Just because conditions are improving, it doesn't mean getting out of here will be totally risk-free. The track will still be quite dodgy. We're all going down in the Land Rover. The local garage can pick your car up later and keep it for collection.' Without giving her a chance for any further objections, he turned away and strode over to the barn where Venna's car and the Land Rover were parked side by side. 'I'll give the engine a run and make sure it's OK while you get breakfast.'

No please or would you mind?, Venna fumed. Just a peremptory order. Yet she found herself moving meekly to obey it.

She cooked a substantial breakfast in case they didn't have time to eat again before they left, then left it to keep warm while she went into the other room to get Gemma up. When she saw her niece she was glad they would probably be leaving today. The child was definitely off colour and inclined to be fretful. She seemed uninterested in her food, and Venna had to coax her to take every mouthful.

'That settles it,' Keir said. 'Somehow we're getting back to civilisation today.' He probably thought it was her fault Gemma wasn't well, Venna thought gloomily, but she was too concerned about the child to spend much time worrying over Keir's apportionment of blame.

'Do you want to see if there's a doctor in Coniston?' he asked.

Venna thought about it, then shook her head.

'No, I'd rather she saw our own doctor, in Southport.'

By midday the Land Rover was packed, and at two o'clock Keir decided conditions were as good as they were going to be that day. Though plenty of snow still lingered, the sky was cloudless and blue, the air crisp and clear as they made their cautious descent of the Forestry track. It was a slow process and, despite her absolute confidence in Keir's abilities, once or twice Venna's heart was in her mouth. To herself she admitted that she was glad he hadn't allowed her to drive her car out. But at last they reached the valley floor and then they were driving through the sparkling sunshine of a perfect winter afternoon.

Winter? But it would soon be spring, Venna realised as they drove south, their belongings now transferred to

Keir's car. As they left the Lake District the snowline gradually receded. Village gardens were filled with flowering bulbs, and birch trees lining the road were ready to burst into leaf. It was as if it had all happened overnight.

Further south still, the first few lambs had already arrived, and Keir slowed so that Venna could point them out to Gemma.

For a moment or two the sight roused the child from her apathy, and above her head Venna and Keir exchanged a relieved smile. But it was still obvious the child was unwell. Consequently they only made one necessary stop en route, and before long they were on the wide approach road that led to Southport and to the area around Hesketh Park where Venna's flat was situated.

'It's too late for evening surgery now,' Venna said worriedly as Keir carried a softly whimpering Gemma upstairs. 'But I really think I ought to call the doctor out.'

'I think you'll find, where a very young child is concerned, he won't object, even if it turns out to be something and nothing.' Keir looked at Venna's tired, anxious face. He put his hand on her arm and gave it a reassuring squeeze. 'Even if it's only for your own peace of mind, I should call him. I'll stay with you until he's been, if you like.'

'Why, where were you going?'

'To book in at a hotel, of course.' Drily, 'I didn't think you'd approve of my staying here.' Strangely, it had never occurred to her that he would do anything else. After all, they had slept in the same house, in the same room even, for several nights.

'I thought you might be determined not to let me out of your sight,' she retorted with something of her usual spirit.

He smiled, and her heart turned over at the engaging sight.

'Oh, I think we understand each other better now, Venna. I don't think you'll pull a silly stroke like running away again, will you? You know now that it's no use, that I'm not going to let you go that easily.' If only he intended that in the way she wished he meant it.

'Now then, let's have a look at the wee lassie!' As Keir had said, the doctor, an elderly Scot with a brisk but kind manner, had made no demur about coming out. And Venna was relieved that she had taken his advice. For during the half-hour wait the child had begun to vomit. As Venna watched anxiously, the doctor sat on the side of the bed and took the child's pulse. He listened to heart and lungs, took her temperature. 'Hmmph!' It was a non-committal sound, and yet to Venna it held a threat. She darted a frightened look at Keir, who had remained in the bedroom.

He moved towards her and her hand was taken in a strong, warm clasp that was obviously meant as reassurance. It had that effect, but it also made her want to move closer to him, to feel the support of his strength in this moment of anxiety. Firmly she resisted the impulse and concentrated on watching the doctor's face, and tried to learn something from his expression.

'I want this wee soul in hospital—tonight,' he said at last.

Despite the warmth of the room, Venna felt herself go cold. Her mouth went dry and she began to shake. With her tongue cleaving to the roof of her mouth, she couldn't speak. It was Keir who asked the question as his hand tightened on hers and drew her firmly against his side.

'What is it, Doctor?' he asked quietly. Though his manner was calm, Venna, attuned to every nuance in the room, was aware of his concern and her alarm grew proportionately. Her fingers gripped his.

'I'm not certain—yet.' The doctor darted a look under shaggy brows at Venna's white, strained face. 'We'll need to run some tests on the bairn, ye ken?' He became brisk. 'Put her a few things together, Miss Leigh. I'll ring for an ambulance.'

'Can't we take her to the hospital ourselves?' Venna found her voice, albeit a faint one.

'Best to let the professionals do it, lassie.' But his manner was kindly. 'You can go along with her, of course.'

Instinctively, Venna turned her head to look up at Keir, a question in her great green eyes.

'I'm coming, too,' he told her, and she gave a little sob of relief. There might be hours of waiting, and she didn't want to be alone with her fears.

The bag with the child's few small needs was soon packed, and it seemed ages, though in reality it was only ten minutes, before the ambulance stopped outside. Wrapped in a red blanket and held in the ambulance man's arms, Gemma looked pathetically small and the tears that had pricked behind Venna's eyes overflowed as she followed the man downstairs.

Inside the vehicle, Keir sat close to her, his arm around her shaking shoulders, his cheek against her bright hair.

'Try not to worry, Venna.' He gave her a rallying little shake. 'It may be nothing serious. You know children do develop these sudden high temperatures for no apparent reason. She may be as right as rain tomorrow.'

She desperately wanted to believe him. But Gemma had never been sick before, and Venna she couldn't quell the uneasy voice of conscience that was telling her this was all her fault. She should never have taken Gemma from a warm home to that bleak Lakeland cottage. In her own selfish concern for the future she had acted irresponsibly. And if it were not the wintry conditions to which she had submitted her baby niece, then it must be some kind of punishment for all the lies and deception of the past few days.

Venna subscribed to no particular religious belief. But her grandmother had been a Christian of the unbending kind, and dogmatic in her conviction that God was an avenging deity who kept strict accounts. Because it had been the best educational establishment available, Venna had been educated at a convent where right and wrong and retribution for the latter had been even more severely underlined. Perhaps, she thought now, there was something in it, after all. She wished there had been someone to whom she could pour out all these doubts and fears. But there was only Keir, and he was the last person to whom she could make her confession.

At the hospital they formed a melancholy procession that hurried through hushed, antiseptic-smelling corridors. To Venna, the odour at once brought back primitive memories of sickness and death, and the fear that had accompanied them. As children, she and Shelagh had been taken to see their mother in hospital during her mercifully brief but terminal illness. Then more recently there had been their grandmother's death.

The nurses put Gemma to bed. Venna was only allowed to hover and watch, feeling more and more helpless. By this time the child's temperature was at danger point, and the efficient night staff went into action. The child was stripped off and covered in cold soaked pads to bring her temperature down.

'Poor little mite,' Venna choked against Keir's shoulder. 'She doesn't understand what's happening to her.'

'I know, I know.' He hugged her consolingly. 'But don't let her see you break down, my dear.' His voice was a little unsteady.

Then the tests began. Venna felt every pain the child went through, but all she could do was hold the small hand and will her niece to survive.

Finally, when it seemed every possible test had been made, the ward sister suggested that Keir and Venna should go home and return next day.

'We'll give her something to make her sleep now, and it will be some hours before we get the results of any tests.'

But Venna was adamant that she was staying, and she and Keir waited for what seemed endless hours in a bare antechamber. To Venna, the room seemed pervaded with the worries and sorrows of others who had waited here like this, perhaps known bereavement. She had to say something to break the taut silence.

'I...I don't know what I'll do,' she croaked, 'if anything happens to Gemma.'

'Nothing's going to happen to her.' Keir put both arms about her this time and pressed her fiery head against his broad chest. 'Just thank God that we didn't have to spend another day in that cottage, that we were within reach of medical help.'

'You...you believe in God, don't you, Keir?' Her voice was muffled against his thick sweater, his warm, masculine smell blotting out the hated odour of hospitals. Although she couldn't tell him everything, neither could she keep off the notion that now haunted her. 'Do...do you believe in...in punishment for wrongdoing?'

He put a hand under her chin and lifted her tear-streaked face so that he could see it.

'Punishment for what wrongdoing?' He studied her expression. 'Yours?' Then, perceptively, 'You believe Gemma's illness is retribution for some act of yours, don't you?' And, as she nodded, 'Because you deprived Tris of his daughter, you believe God is about to deprive *you*?' That wasn't quite it, but it was near enough. Again she nodded. 'What nonsense, my dear,' he said gently. 'That isn't the way things work at all. The God I believe in is a merciful one.' And, sternly, as she parted her lips to speak, 'I forbid you to think that way, Venna. Gemma is going to be all right.' Again he pulled her into his arms. 'Maybe you don't have any faith in the power of prayer,' he said against her hair, 'but I do, enough faith for both of us.'

Comforted in some measure, she allowed him to go on holding her, and wearied by the day's events and her anxieties she dozed fitfully in his arms, waking occasionally to the reassurance of his presence, his murmured calming words.

Lulled by his confident manner into some measure of security, it came as a worse shock when a few hours later a grave-faced doctor came to tell them the results of Gemma's tests. He spoke to Keir.

'So far, Mr...?'

'Trevelyan,' Keir supplied.

'So far all the tests have proved negative. But we're investigating the possibility now of meningitis.'

'Meningitis!' Venna had jumped to her feet at the sight of the doctor. Now she swayed dangerously and grasped at Keir for support. It was instantly given, his arm about her waist.

'Now try not to worry, Mrs Trevelyan.' Venna was too distraught to correct the form of address. 'The type of meningitis children of this age contract almost always responds to treatment with antibiotics.'

'Almost always,' Venna repeated dully. The qualification did nothing to reassure her.

'Again it will be several hours before we can tell you anything definite. Mr Trevelyan, may I suggest you take your wife home so she can get some rest? Call us later this morning. If there are any developments, naturally we'll contact you immediately.'

'I think that would be best, Venna,' Keir told her gently. 'You can't do any good staying here.'

'I'm not going,' Venna sobbed. 'How can I rest when Gemma might be dangerously ill?'

'Perhaps you could prescribe some sleeping-pills,' Keir suggested to the doctor.

'No!' It was a high-pitched cry of protest. 'I don't want sleeping-pills. I'm not looking for a cop-out, so that I can forget what's happening.' Venna was almost beside herself with nervous tension. 'I want to know what's going on, every minute. I want to be with Gemma. I'm her only... I'm her mother!'

'All right,' Keir said soothingly, 'no sleeping-pills. But I'm going to insist on taking you home. Gemma's asleep. She's in good hands and it won't be any help to anyone if you crack up.'

Mentally she could resist him, physically she could not, and he must have known that, for with a sudden swift movement he swept her up in his arms and, despite his uneven gait, carried her swiftly towards the exit. She couldn't make a noisy scene in a hospital full of sick people. Besides, she was too tired and too emotionally exhausted. Her head against his shoulder, she cried quietly and continued to cry in the taxi all the way back to the flat.

He carried her upstairs, setting her down only while she took the door-key out of her handbag.

'Maybe you won't take drugs,' he told her as he steered her through the flat towards her bedroom, 'but I recommend a hot bath, a warm drink and some aspirin. The bath first.'

'I can't!' She shook her head wearily. 'I just can't be bothered. Nothing seems to matter except Gemma.'

'You need something to relax you,' he insisted. 'You're as taut as a bowstring. You're going to have that bath if I have to put you into it myself.' He set her down on the side of the bed and strode into the adjoining bathroom, and seconds later she heard the sound of running water. 'Now!' he stood in the doorway. 'What's it to be? Are you going to undress yourself or do I have to?'

'No!' She moved with surprising quickness for someone who had just been on the verge of utter collapse. 'I'll do it myself.'

'Good girl!' He nodded his dark head approvingly. 'That's more like the Venna I've come to know. While you're in the bath, I'll put some milk on to heat.'

The bath did help to relax her a little. But it was weakening, too. Alone, without Keir's brusque, matter-of-fact sanity to uphold her, her fears took on more menacing aspect. Soon she had convinced herself that the next news she would hear would be of Gemma's death, and the tears slid down her face as she lay limply in the rapidly cooling water.

'Venna! Venna!' The bathroom door flew open and only then did she realise Keir had been calling her for some time. 'God dammit! What are you playing at?' he snapped as instinctively she folded her arms across her breasts. 'I thought you'd passed out or something.' Then his keen eyes saw the tears and at once his manner altered. 'Oh, my dear!' His voice was husky. 'You mustn't cry like that. You'll make yourself ill. Come on! Let's get you out of there.' He opened the airing-cupboard and took out the towel she'd forgotten to put ready. 'Stand up!'

Apathetically she obeyed him, stood unresisting while he enfolded her in the towel's warmth then briskly began to rub her dry. He made her sit on the side of the bath while he dried her feet.

Somehow it didn't seem to matter, Venna thought through her dull fog of unhappiness, that he should see her entirely naked like this. The service he was performing for her was an entirely impersonal one, as though she were a tired child. A child. Like Gemma. A stifled sob escaped her and he looked up quickly.

'Venna,' he pleaded, 'don't!'

'Oh, Keir,' she said, 'what am I going to do?'

He stood up, then took her in his arms and held her closely. The towel fell unheeded to the floor.

'Go on hoping, praying, believing,' he told her gently. 'It's all any of us can do. Just try to remember, Venna, that you're not alone in all this. I'm here. Hold on to me if it helps.'

'It does,' she said gratefully.

He put a hand under her chin and lifted her still tear-wet face. He bent his head and his lips brushed softly over her wet cheeks, her damp eyelids. It was a gentle exploration and, as she didn't shrink from it, his mouth moved down to cover hers, and for a moment she knew its consolatory warmth. Somewhere deep in her icy misery something stirred fugitively and fluttered awake. Then he moved uneasily and put her from him.

'We'd better get you into bed,' he told her. His voice was somewhat throaty. He stooped to pick up the neglected towel and wrapped it round her once more. 'I've put a hot-water bottle in your bed,' he told her. 'Go and get your nightclothes on while I fetch your drink. It will probably need warming up again.'

She pulled on the garment that lay on the bed. The nightdress Keir had put out wasn't really suitable for winter wear, but she couldn't be bothered to hunt for her pyjamas. She turned back the quilt and was about to climb into bed, but she stopped short at the sight of the hot-water bottle. It hadn't occurred to her when he had mentioned it. They only possessed one hot-water bottle. Gemma's. At the sight of it in its furry rabbit-shaped case her stomach lurched. There were no tears this time, only dry, shuddering sobs that seemed to rack the entire length of her slim body as she crouched on the side of the bed, holding the bottle.

'What it it? I . . .' Keir, with her glass of warm milk in his hand, hurried into the bedroom. With his quick perception he took in the cause of her distress. 'I'm sorry,' he said. 'Perhaps it was tactless of me, but it was the only one I could find.'

'It . . . it's not your fault,' she gasped between sobs. And as he bent to remove the hot-water bottle, she cried 'No,' and held it tightly clasped against her breast.

'Get into bed.' Gently he urged her beneath the quilt and drew it up to cover her. 'Now take these.' He handed her two aspirins. 'And drink your milk.' He stood over her while she obeyed. 'Now lie back and close your eyes. At least try to sleep.' And, as her wide-eyed over-bright stare still held his, he murmured, 'Venna?'

'You . . . you won't go away, will you?' She whispered the words supplicatingly. Fatigue and fear had overcome her normal self-reliance.

For answer he sat down on the edge of the bed and took one of her hands in both of his.

'I'll sit here, shall I, until you go to sleep?'

'Please. But . . . but you won't go then? You won't go to a hotel?' Her lips trembled at the thought that he might leave her alone.

'No.' His throat worked strangely for a moment. 'No, I'll be around, Venna, for as long as you want me. You can count on that.'

CHAPTER SIX

SHE was so warm and comfortable. She was enveloped in a kind of security she had never known before. Venna stirred in her sleep and snuggled blissfully closer to the source of warmth and strength.

'Venna!' A deep voice speaking her name seemed to want to draw her up and out of this safe cocoon. But she didn't want to wake up. When she woke, the leaden heaviness that hovered threateningly would descend on her chest again, banishing this utter contentment. She couldn't remember what the heaviness portended. She didn't want to remember.

'Venna!' The voice was insistent. It was familiar. It was a voice she trusted—and loved. She opened her eyes and stared wonderingly.

Keir was lying on the bed beside her. He was still fully dressed, and besides that the thickness of the quilt divided them. But apart from that he was as close to her as he could be, one arm thrown protectively around her, his rugged, swarthy face only inches away. She felt a surge of sensuality engulf her in its warmth.

For a bemused moment she stared at him, her lips slightly parted, breathlessly aware, loving him, wanting him. Then with a sickening jolt she remembered, and the hovering heaviness descended. Her mouth trembled.

'What time is it?' Despite the misery that had immediately overwhelmed her, she tried to keep her voice steady. He must be sick to death of her crying all over him.

He raised his arm to consult an expensive gold watch that banded a wrist darkly coated with fine soft hair.

'Almost twelve.'

'Twelve! Midday! Oh, Keir, how *could* you? How could you let me sleep in so late? Gemma...'

'The hospital promised to get in touch if there was any change, remember? And you needed that sleep.' But he rolled over and got to his feet, came round to her side of the bed. He proffered her dressing-gown. 'Here, put this on and then I'll phone the hospital.' He held the garment while she slipped her arms into it. Then he pulled the front edges together, drawing her towards him as he did so. So briefly that she could almost have imagined it, she felt his lips brush her forehead. 'Try not to worry, Venna.'

She longed to put her arms about Keir's waist and bury her head on that broad chest, to feel his arms go reassuringly about her. But today, she admonished herself, she must behave with more maturity. Goodness knew what he had thought of her behaviour yesterday. Yesterday she'd at least had the excuse of being over-tired. Gemma's illness on top of that had reduced her to the clinging, tearful creature she had been. If she wanted Keir to think her a competent guardian for Gemma, she must show more strength and resolution in adversity.

'*I'll* telephone,' she said firmly.

It seemed ages before the switchboard answered her call, then ages again before she was put through to the ward sister. As she listened her face brightened. But gradually blank bewilderment replaced the happy expression, and Keir saw the colour drain from her cheeks. She returned the receiver to its rest, then slumped down into a chair and looked up at him, her green eyes dark with misery.

'What is it?' Then, urgently, as she didn't answer, 'Venna, for God's sake, don't keep me in suspense. What is it?'

'I . . . I don't understand,' she said faintly. 'At first I thought it was good news. They said she hasn't got meningitis. But then they said she's very ill indeed, and something about needing an emergency operation. They're calling in a specialist.' She jumped up, then had to grab hold of Keir for support as her legs trembled beneath her. 'I have to go to her,' she gasped frantically. 'I have to be there.'

'Of course you do,' Keir said soothingly. With his usual efficiency, he took charge. 'Get dressed,' he ordered. 'I'll get you there as quickly as possible.'

Afterwards Venna couldn't remember putting on her clothes. The becoming peacock-blue jumper and skirt were the first things that came to hand as her trembling hands fumbled in wardrobe and drawers. Her mind was racing ahead, crossing a thousand troubled bridges before she came to them.

Keir drove swiftly through the town to reach the hospital in what must have been record time. A hand under Venna's elbow, he propelled her through the corridors. She was numbly aware of his presence, grateful for his strength, without which she might never have reached their objective.

It was Keir who asked all the right questions and seemed to understand the answers. Venna's brain was fogged with an incomprehension induced by fear. An X-ray had revealed an unindentified swelling in Gemma's stomach.

'It looks like a big bag of air,' Keir explained carefully to Venna. 'They think it might be a blockage in the intestine. The specialist will be here very soon.'

'Can we see her?'

'Not just now. She's on her way down to theatre.'

'Oh, Keir!' Despite all her earlier resolutions, she clung to his arm, frantic with worry. 'Is she . . . is she going to be all right?'

'I don't know, Venna.' He held her closely. 'I wish I could give you an answer. But we just have to wait and see—and hope.'

'So much for your precious God and your prayers!' Venna exploded. 'And will you still believe in Him if he lets Gemma die?'

Wisely he did not attempt a reply to this outburst of baffled, angry misery. He simply continued to hold her, rocking her gently, one hand smoothing the lustrous wine-coloured hair.

They knew when the specialist went into the theatre. Then for two hours they waited.

Keir suggested to a restless Venna that they walk around the hospital grounds, but she refused to leave the building. Even so, she could not sit still but paced the small waiting-room until its dimensions were indelibly printed upon her mind. She drank the tea a sympathetic nurse brought her, but choked over the accompanying biscuit.

At last the news came. It had been a long and delicate operation. The swelling the X-rays had revealed had turned out to be Gemma's right kidney, where a blockage had caused urine to build up. No wonder the child had been in such pain.

They were taken into the recovery room, where a heart-rending sight met their eyes. Gemma looked so frail and tiny. Endless tubes and pipes went in and out of her little body. At the sight of her small niece, Venna was once more unable to hold back the tears.

The operation had been a complete success, the surgeon told them.

'So she'll be all right now?' Keir demanded. His voice sounded unsteady and, looking at him, Venna thought she detected a glint of moisture on his dark lashes as she stared down at the child. He really cared, she thought wonderingly.

'Eventually, we hope.' The doctor was cautious. 'There'll be a recovery period, of course.'

'I want to stay with her,' Venna said. 'She'll be so frightened when she wakes up if I'm not there.'

No problem, she was told. Arrangements could be made for a mother and toddler room adjoining the main ward.

'We'll take it in turns to sit with her,' Keir said. 'You ought to go back to the flat occasionally for some proper rest.'

But Venna shook her fiery head vigorously.

'I couldn't bear that. I want to be able to see her, to know she's all right.' She didn't even look at him, she had eyes only for Gemma now.

'I see,' Keir said shortly. 'In that case, if you don't need *me*, there's not much point in my hanging about here, or in Southport. I may as well go down to London for a few days and catch up on some neglected work.'

'Oh!' Now he did have all her attention. Somehow Venna hadn't expected that. She'd had the reassuring notion that Keir would still be there, in the background, but not too far away if she needed him. Now she reproached herself for her thoughtlessness. Of course he would want to get on with his own life. She'd caused him enough trouble. He probably couldn't afford to be away from his estate agency business any longer. Besides, she had no right to expect it of him. Gemma was his main concern, not her. Though he seemed content to leave his niece's welfare to the hospital now.

'Of course you must go.' She tried to sound unconcerned. 'I don't usually behave as I did yesterday. I can manage perfectly well.'

'Right,' he spoke curtly again. 'I'll leave you my telephone number.' He searched his inside breast pocket, then scribbled some figures on the back of an old envelope. 'Keep me informed of Gemma's progress, won't you?'

'Of course!'

She didn't know why, but she'd half expected he might kiss her goodbye. When he left with just a brief nod and a half-salute, she felt ridiculously bereft. He had been so kind and supportive throughout the worst hours of Gemma's illness, she'd felt they had become friends, if nothing else, drawn together by their shared anxiety. Now, suddenly, he had retreated into reserve—a stranger once more, and she didn't know what to think.

There was plenty of time for thinking during the next few days and nights as she watched endlessly at Gemma's bedside, though not of Keir. For the majority of the time the child slept, but Venna could not rest properly. She felt she must keep up her vigil night and day. When Gemma slept Venna dozed in her chair. And when Gemma was awake the child was uncharacteristically demanding and fretful, puzzled by the various attachments to her small body.

But day by day the wounds healed and stitches were removed, and when it seemed certain that Gemma was out of danger Venna found her thoughts turning more and more to Keir Trevelyan.

The envelope on which he had scribbled his telephone number had provided some food for reflection as well as further information about Keir himself. The envelope was empty, but the form of address on the envelope told her that Keir had degrees in law and economics and was the managing director of a company known as Pednolva Enterprises. The London address Venna recognised as being a very prestigious area.

A couple of times she'd telephoned the number Keir had given her, intending to give him a progress report. But each time a cool secretarial voice had told her he was not available.

If it were not for the tireless way Keir had searched for her in the first place, his persistence in following her and Gemma to the Lake District, Venna would have been

tempted to think he'd gone out of their lives for good.
Certainly, it would be more natural for her to hope so.
His disappearance from the scene would have ensured
her total possession of Gemma. But she didn't want to
lose touch with Keir Trevelyan. Even though she was
nothing to him, she knew he had come to mean everything to her. She had refused to marry him, but she felt
that she would be happy enough just to be involved in
some small way in his life.

A few days before Gemma was due to be discharged
from hospital, Keir entered the little hospital room.

Venna was dozing as usual in her chair at the side of
the child's bed. Though the staff had insisted she get
some fresh air from time to time, she had stayed out of
doors for the minimum period only, uneasy all the time
she was away from her baby niece. Consequently her
normally fresh complexion was dull, her face drawn and
her green eyes violet-shadowed from too little sleep.

At the sound of Keir's voice she started, and as she
turned her head towards him and saw the dark, blunt
features so dear to her she felt the blood race feverishly
in her pulses. Joy welled up in her and she wanted to
jump up and fling herself into his arms, but she knew
she must restrain the impulse. She thought she knew only
too well how he would react—with distaste and
embarrassment.

She was glad she hadn't made such an idiot of herself
when he said with blunt ferocity, 'Good God, Venna,
what have you been doing to yourself? You look awful!'

'Thanks!' she muttered, and she felt her eyelids
pricking. She hadn't seen him or heard from him for
days. Did his first words to her have to be angry and
derogatory?

It didn't improve things when he turned immediately
on his heel and strode from the room, without saying
where he was going or even whether he intended coming
back. Miserably, Venna hunched her shoulders and re-

turned to her intent watch upon Gemma. After a moment or two her eyelids drooped heavily once more.

The next thing she knew was she was being forcibly dragged from her chair and Keir was shaking her.

'You little fool! Staff nurse tells me you've been here all this time, that you've only been home once, and then only for an hour. You've had scarcely any fresh air, exercise or sleep, and you've been eating like a bird. What are you trying to do? End up in a hospital bed yourself?'

'I'm all right,' she said. But she felt weak and shaky, and she knew it wasn't entirely due to his proximity, though that was having its usual powerful effect upon her.

'You're far from all right,' he contradicted. 'Here, put your coat on.' He snatched it up from the back of the chair and forced her unwilling arms into the sleeves. 'You're coming with me.' He began to propel her towards the door.

'No,' she protested. 'I can't.' She began to struggle, but his grip was inexorable. 'Gemma might wake and miss me. She . . .'

'The nurses tell me Gemma is almost fully recovered now and quite accustomed to them. They're going to move her into the main children's ward now. She won't come to any harm without you for twenty-four hours.'

'Twenty-four hours! I can't leave her that long.'

'You can and you will.' They had reached the door by now.

Outside in the corridor she succeeded in freeing herself from the iron clasp of his fingers. She faced him angrily.

'You've no right to behave in this high-handed manner. I can run my life perfectly well without your interference. In fact,' she spoke out of the lonely brooding of the past days, 'I'm surprised you even bothered to come back to Southport.'

'Is that what you were hoping for when you didn't telephone me?' He had grasped her arm again and was practically frog-marching her towards the exit. He sounded angry. 'You were only concerned with your own worries, weren't you? What about mine? If I hadn't rung the hospital myself from time to time I'd have no idea how Gemma was.'

'I *did* telephone you!' she exclaimed indignantly. 'But you were never available.'

'Did you give the switchboard your name?'

'No, I . . .'

'I left instructions that you were to be put through to me immediately,' he said with exasperation, 'even if I was in conference, which I mostly was. If you'd told the operator who you were instead of meekly accepting . . .'

'Oh, stop it! Stop it!' Venna exclaimed brokenly. She was just about at the end of her tether, she realised. 'Stop nagging me. Do you think I liked not being able to speak to you, to talk to you about Gemma? I've been so worried. I . . .'

'About Gemma?' he stopped by his car and turned to look down at her. His voice was more gentle. 'But when I rang they told me she'd been on the mend from the day after the operation. Surely they told you that?'

'Yes, but . . .' In fact, what she had nearly blurted out was that she been worried she might never see *him* again.

'But you're a constitutional worrier!' he reproached. He ushered her into the car and went round to the driver's side. He sat sideways in the seat and looked wonderingly at her, taking in afresh the pallor of her lovely face, the deep hollows under the green eyes. He shook his dark head wonderingly. 'I would never have believed it if I hadn't met you. I expected a woman who would deliberately choose single parenthood to be tougher, more aggressive, more self-reliant, certainly not a worrier.'

She shook her head almost in bewilderment.

'I'm not usually like this, honestly I'm not. But until you've loved someone you don't know what worry is, especially when you're afraid you might be going to lose them.' Her low-voiced words held a double meaning that he knew nothing about.

'That's very true, Venna.'

'How would you know?' she asked wearily. 'You don't believe in love.'

He started the engine.

'Nevertheless I . . .'

'Where are you taking me?' she wanted to know.

'Back to the flat. You're going to take a bath while I rustle us up a meal, and then you're going to bed.'

She wished he were coming to bed with her, she found herself thinking, and blushed hotly, glad that his attention was now on the traffic-congested road. If she wasn't going to betray her feelings for him she must avoid thoughts like that—at least in his presence.

Motorists, attracted by a sudden spell of almost summer-like weather, were streaming into Southport, headed for the mile-long Lord Street and its shops, the beach and the parks.

It was a lovely day, Venna realised. During her voluntary incarceration, March had gone and April was here.

With the sun shining warmly through the car windscreen on to her face, she felt suddenly uplifted, exalted. She knew it was not just Gemma's steady recovery or the weather that was making her feel this way. Keir was back. For the moment, that was enough. And there was the promise of more days in his company when they took Gemma to see his mother. She would snatch at such moments as these and live each one to the full while they lasted.

'I suppose you haven't given any more thought to the future?' Keir asked as they neared Hesketh Park. It was almost as if he'd read her mind. These last few days, since Gemma's recovery had been certain, she had thought about nothing else.

'I've thought about it, yes,' she said warily.

'And you haven't changed your mind? About the role you intend to play?'

'I'm coming to Cornwall as Gemma's nanny, if that's what you mean.'

'You almost agreed to marry me once,' he reminded her, his tone neutral.

'No, I didn't. I agreed to think about it.' And she hadn't been in love with him then. That made all the difference.

'I see,' and now he said it curtly. 'I thought recent events might have changed your mind. Very well. We'll go down to Cornwall as soon as Gemma is well enough to travel.'

Keir was no slouch as a cook, Venna thought, when a couple of hours later she sat down to a meal with more appetite than she had expected. While she bathed, Keir had visited the small local shops and produced a very creditable steak and french fries. The accompanying wine made her feel slightly light-headed, or maybe that was just Keir's presence, she mused.

'It's not exactly cordon bleu,' he'd apologised as he set her plate before her.

'It's delicious. Obviously you're a man of hidden talents.' Her green eyes sparkled out of a face to which a warm bath had brought a rosy glow.

'There are a lot of things about me that you don't know,' he said gravely. There was a moment or two of silence in which Venna, every nerve-end alive to his presence, thought she must be imagining the growing sense of tension. 'Did you miss me at all this last week, Venna?' he asked suddenly.

At a loss for an evasive answer, for the exact truth was unthinkable, she looked warily at him.

'No,' he supplied an answer himself. 'I don't suppose you did. You had all you wanted in that hospital room.'

His eyes were intent, but not upon her face. Following their direction, Venna realised that the neck of her dressing-gown had fallen open and that the gap had revealed the swell of creamy-skinned breasts and the mysterious shadowy cleft between them. She hadn't bothered to dress after her bath, since Keir was so insistent that she should take a rest. Now heat invaded her whole body, and hastily she remedied her robe's deficiencies.

Her hurried reaction seemed to recall him from some deep absorption.

'I'm sorry,' he said huskily. 'I didn't mean to embarrass you, but you do have the most incredibly lovely body.' And, as she made a little sound of denial, he went on, 'Don't forget,' his tone was warmly reminiscent, 'I have seen more of you than that.'

As if she *could* forget! She only wished those moments when she had stood naked in his arms could have been on a happier occasion, that they could have held a deeper meaning.

'I can quite see,' he went on broodingly, 'why Tris went half mad trying to find you. You have a deceptive appearance of sexuality. Your eyes, your mouth, the curves of your body all speak of a woman ripe for love. And yet . . .'

'Keir, please,' Venna said pleadingly, 'don't!' She didn't want to talk about love and desire because she was desperately tired, more tired perhaps than Keir realised, and she didn't feel up to fencing with him. She might give something away, reveal her heightened reactions to him. He misunderstood.

'Oh, don't worry!' He stood up abruptly and pushed back his chair. His voice lost its warmth, took on a harsh intensity. 'I know you find any discussion of sexuality distasteful.'

'It's not that,' she protested. It was becoming increasingly hard to maintain the image of the frigid creature he thought her, especially here alone with him, with her whole body craving for the feel of his arms about her. She and Shelagh had never discussed the matter, but Venna honestly didn't think her half-sister had been frigid. Her choice had been prompted rather by an over-sensitive nature that feared exposing itself to hurt.

But Keir didn't seem to be listening to her. His intelligent forehead was creased into a frown.

'What beats me, even given your motive, is how you ever brought yourself to be intimate with my brother. Did you have to grit your teeth, Venna? Did you emulate the ignorant Victorian bride? Did you lie back and think of England?' He was pacing the room now as if something would not let him rest. With every question his voice had grown harder.

She hadn't heard him speak with that bitter, sardonic note for a long time. It grated on nerves still raw from the fatigue and anxieties of the past days. It seemed Keir still bore her a grudge on his brother's behalf, she thought sadly. Any hopes that he might have softened towards her were dashed. With a sudden gesture of rejection she pushed away her half-empty plate.

'You haven't finished!' he accused. 'Eat it!'

'Neither have you,' she pointed out. 'Anyway, I've had enough!' she told him wearily. 'Enough food and enough of you and your... your high-handed behaviour, your insults.' She stood up, her small chin tilted in a brave attempt at defiance.

'Insults?' He queried the word, one dark eyebrow lifted. 'Since when was the truth insulting? You've never made any secret of the fact that you didn't want a man in your bed for any other purpose than...'

'Stop it! Stop it!' She put her hands over her ears to shut out the undeserved censure. 'You've got it all wrong. You don't understand. It wasn't...'

'You want me to believe it wasn't like that?' he said incredulously. His interruption had only just saved her from blurting out the truth.

He moved towards her, and no matter how tightly she pressed her hands to her head she could not shut out his voice, the sudden urgent note it contained. 'Am I to understand that you *did* enjoy sex with my brother? That it's not obnoxious to you?'

'You can think what you like,' she flared. 'I couldn't care less.'

'But *I* could! I want to know, not think!' Two strong hands dragged hers down to her sides. 'What *is* the truth, Venna? If you don't find sex distasteful, would you care to prove it—to *me*?'

He didn't give her a chance to answer. Before she could guess his purpose, his lips took hers in a sudden, savage kiss. The movements of his mouth on hers were like those of a man starved.

She couldn't think why he was behaving like this all of a sudden. He had once admitted to finding her sexually attractive. But he'd never before shown any inclination to give rein to that attraction. Despite his belief that she was the woman who had destroyed his brother, and in spite of an underlying animosity, he had been courteous and gentle. Such kisses as he had bestowed on her recently had been as chaste as those he gave Gemma.

Now he was kissing her almost brutally, forcing her lips apart, invading them with his tongue, the pressure of his teeth bruising her soft mouth. He was holding her so close that she couldn't help knowing of his arousal.

At first she resisted but, insidiously, the feel of his hard vitality against her stomach was creating an answering response within her. As she allowed her hands to follow their impulse to creep around his neck, she felt his heart-beat accelerate. Her own was deafening in her ears. Feverishly she began to return the growing insistence of his kisses. Waves of feeling rippled through her as passion mounted between them.

One of his hands had found the opening of her dressing-gown, and caressingly he shaped the breasts that were surprisingly generous for someone of her small stature. His fingers stroked and cajoled nipples already hard with desire. And before long his mouth was following where his hands had led.

'You're beautiful, Venna,' she heard him say at last, his voice muffled against her breasts. 'You know I want to make love to you? God knows how I want to!'

And *she* wanted *him*. She had never given herself to any man. But she knew she would gladly, willingly give herself to Keir Trevelyan. Her body was shaking in helpless response to the sensuality that flowed between them, and she gave a strangled whimper of protest when, as suddenly as he had grabbed her, he thrust her away from him. For a moment he stood looking down at her, his grey eyes burning steel in his dark-complexioned face. Then he swung away and took a step or two across the room.

'I'm sorry,' he said gruffly, not looking at her, so that he did not see the pleading hands she stretched out to him. 'I didn't intend anything like that to happen.' He passed a hand that trembled slightly through the thick, greying thatch of his hair. 'Just for a moment your whole attitude maddened me. I've never taken any woman without caring. But for a moment I wanted to...to...' He gestured helplessly.

'To punish me, I suppose,' she said tremulously. 'That's what you've wanted to do all along, isn't it? That's why you'd vowed to track Sh...me down.' He couldn't know he'd succeeded beyond his expectations, that she was now undergoing the most severe punishment fate could have devised.

'You're wrong, Venna, but if that's what you want to think...' His broad-shouldered shrug was a masterpiece of indifference. He seemed to have regained control of himself much faster than she had.

But she supposed that must be because—despite the physical allure he felt—basically he disliked and despised her. He had put it in a nutshell when he'd said he had never taken any woman without caring. For caring read liking, she reminded herself. Keir didn't believe in any more tender emotion. All he felt for her was desire, she thought, lust, call it what you would. Whereas she had love to deepen the increasing attraction he held for her.

She turned her back on him so that he could not see her face, and moved towards the bedroom door. She suddenly needed to get away from him. She needed time to think.

'Since you made me come home for a rest,' she told him, 'I might as well get some sleep.'

He didn't argue with her. Instead he announced grimly, 'And I think I'll take a walk.'

It was easy enough to declare her intention of sleeping, Venna discovered, harder by far actually to carry it out.

Behind her determinedly closed eyelids she saw pictures of Keir Trevelyan in all his many moods as vividly as if he stood before her. She had seen him angry, she had seen him icily indifferent. Now she had seen his swarthy face and his grey eyes fired by desire. His kisses had stirred into life sensations that would not let her rest. The whole of her sensitised body was consumed by impossible yearnings. Her tired brain toyed with dreams that would never be realised. But at last, mercifully, exhaustion claimed her.

When she woke some hours later it was already dark outside and a dismayed glance at her watch told her she had missed the hospital's evening visiting-time. Now Gemma was in the main ward, Venna's access to her niece would be more restricted.

She got up, showered, then dressed in jeans and a thick, high-necked pullover. She wasn't going to chance provoking Keir's male instincts again.

She hadn't heard him return. But he was in the living-room, reading a copy of the *Visiter*, the local paper. At her entrance he looked up and greeted her calmly. Quite as if earlier events had not occurred, she thought, wishing she could control the blood that had rushed to her cheeks at the sight of him.

'I've been to see Gemma. She's OK and enjoying the company of other children.'

'You might have woken me up in time to go too,' Venna said, resenting such high-handedness.

'I didn't come back to the flat first. I went for a long walk. When I found it had taken me near the hospital I decided to call in.'

'Goodness!' she exclaimed involuntarily. 'You *did* walk a long way.'

'I had a great deal of thinking to do.' It was dourly said, and he didn't volunteer any more than that. Venna was left with the inescapable conclusion that his thoughts must have been very absorbing indeed. She wondered if any of them had concerned her, then discounted the idea. Most likely he had business worries. And no wonder, spending so much time in the north-west, when his firm was in London. His next words confirmed her belief.

'We'll be going down to London before we go on to Cornwall. I must look in at my office for a couple of days. The specialist saw Gemma this afternoon. They'll be discharging her pretty soon.'

'Surely she won't be able to travel immediately?'

'I don't see why not. In a large, comfortable car on the motorway the journey will be an easy one. She'll probably sleep most of the way.'

'Are you . . . are you staying in Southport until then?'

He raised a quizzical eyebrow at her.

'Trying to get rid of me? Hard luck! I certainly didn't drive all this way just for an overnight stay. But don't worry!' His voice hardened. 'While I was out I booked myself into a hotel. I didn't think you'd want me here after what occurred this afternoon. And if we were to stay here alone together,' he electrified her by saying, 'I couldn't guarantee it wouldn't happen again.'

'Oh!' Somehow she'd expected he *would* stay at the flat. But, given his warning, she supposed it was better that he shouldn't. Even so, she felt decidedly downcast. 'So I won't be seeing you, then, until we leave?'

'I didn't say that!' He indicated the paper he'd been reading. 'There seems to be plenty to do in Southport.' And Venna's heart lifted as he added, 'I thought you might care to show me around.'

That was how they passed the intervening time. At night there was live entertainment at the Arts Centre or at one of the theatres. They discovered they shared a taste for humour and light operetta.

By day they did a lot of walking. Despite his limp, Keir was an indefatigable walker, and at times he had to moderate his pace to accommodate Venna's shorter stride. There was no pavement pounding of Lord Street, however. Keir had a male dislike of shops and shopping.

Instead they toured the parks. Hesketh Park, with its unusual shape and contours that made it seem larger than it actually was. The Botanic Gardens, with its museum of Victoriana and Southport history. Keir, Venna discovered, was not too sophisticated to take pleasure in feeding the ducks. There was the beach too, where it was possible to walk the coastline south from Southport, striking off at Freshfield through a pine-wooded nature reserve and returning to Southport by rail.

After a week of being virtually immured in hospital, the fresh air and exercise restored not only Venna's spirits but her natural healthy bloom. She became rosy-cheeked and bright-eyed once more, slept soundly at night, even if her dreams were filled by images of Keir Trevelyan.

She owed part of her renewed cheerfulness to Keir's attitude towards her. His manner was consistently natural and friendly. He was a good conversationalist with informed and interesting opinions on any subject she cared to name. He attempted no familiarities, not even taking her arm to cross roads, until Venna's highly attuned senses were starved for just his slightest touch.

He was a keen sportsman, and in his time, he told her, had played rugby football, tennis and squash.

'I used to ski, too,' he added. 'But that had to go when I broke my leg in a couple of places.' So that was why he limped. She'd often wondered, but hadn't liked to ask. 'So these days I stick mainly to golf.'

One afternoon he hired a set of golf-clubs and coaxed Venna into caddying for him on the municipal golf course.

'I've often thought I'd like to play,' Venna confessed. 'But there seems to be such a mystique about it. And snob value. I've always thought it was a game for the idle rich. But you must be able to afford to play regularly,' she said when she discovered his impressively low handicap.

'Yes, I can just about afford it!' She couldn't think what he seemed to find so immensely amusing.

There were not many players out that day, and on one green Keir persuaded Venna to try her hand at putting. To her delight she discovered she had quite an aptitude for it, and a good eye for direction and pace.

On the next tee he suggested she attempt to drive down the fairway. This proved to be considerably more difficult. The ball flew in totally unexpected directions. Or, more frustratingly, it moved only inches from its original position.

'It's useless,' she despaired, handing him the club. 'I just haven't got the strength to hit it all that way.'

'Nonsense! It's not just a matter of strength. It's the angle at which the face of the club hits the ball. Here, let me show you.' He gave her back the club, placing her hands in the correct position on the shaft. Then he stood behind her, his arms encircling her as he demonstrated the swing. 'Now keep your eye on the ball, all the time,' he commanded. 'Keep your head down. And as you swing back put all your weight on your right foot. Then, as you actually hit the ball, transfer your weight to the left foot and follow through.'

These and other totally incomprehensible instructions assailed her ears. Not incomprehensible because Venna was unintelligent, but because her brain was clouded by her body's reactions to his closeness. It was the first time he'd touched her since that afternoon when he'd returned from London and forcibly removed her from Gemma's hospital bedside.

Now she was aware of the masculine hardness of his body pressed close against hers, the strength of the hands covering hers, the warmth of his breath against her cheek. All coherent thought fled, and with it all pretence at concentration. The club went slack in her hands and she stood, motionless, except for the uncontrollable sensual quivers that rippled through her.

She knew the instant he became aware of her reaction. She felt him stiffen. Heard his breath catch in his throat. The club thudded to the turf. His enfolding arms tightened about her and his lips sought the sensitive area of skin just behind and below her ear.

'Venna!' he groaned. Just her name and nothing more.

Venna swallowed. Involuntarily her eyes closed, and she turned in the circle of his arms, hers going about his waist, her face lifted mutely awaiting his kiss.

When it did not come, her drugged eyelids fluttered open to find him staring down at her, an odd expression on his face.

'You've chosen the darnedest moment to make me aware of you. Or is that why?' he challenged. 'Is it because you feel safe out here in the open, where we can be interrupted?'

He made it sound as though she were a deliberate tease, she thought indignantly. At once she tried to move away, but he wouldn't let her.

'Or is it . . .' He cleared his throat which was suddenly husky. 'Is it that you're learning not to be afraid of me, of your body's instincts?'

An exaggerated cough alerted them to the fact they were no longer alone. A party of three men had caught them up and were waiting to tee off. With a polite gesture Keir invited them to play through.

'I think we'll call it a day,' he told Venna. 'Suddenly, somehow, I don't feel like golf any more. But I think there's hope for you yet.'

'As a golfer, you mean?'

His craggy features broke up into their rare but attractive smile.

'Oh, yes. I think there's hope for that, too!'

CHAPTER SEVEN

As they walked back to the clubhouse they were both silent at first, occupied with their own thoughts. Venna felt shaken, dazed by the strength of her own desires, the knowledge of his. Then Keir stopped, took her hand in his, the ball of his thumb gently massaging her palm.

'Shall we go back to the flat, Venna?' he asked her huskily. 'You know I want to make love to you, and I believe you want me, too. Don't you?' he said insistently, when she made no answer.

She swallowed and, unable to meet his eyes, she stared down at the smooth turf beneath her feet.

'I...I can't, Keir.' She did want him—desperately. But there was more to it than that. As long as she resisted the satisfying of that need she was still her own woman, still retained her self-respect.

But if she gave in to his importuning she would be utterly, hopelessly lost. Physically for a while there might be release. But emotionally? Never!

'Can't, or won't?' he asked almost savagely. Then, before she could frame an answer, 'Are you going to spend the rest of your life like this, just because of something that happened to your mother? Are you going to go on denying yourself one of life's most natural, most pleasurable enjoyments? You're not your mother, Venna. And I'm me, not one of the men who maltreated her. Have you any conception at all of what you're missing?'

If only she hadn't. Her body ached with the pain of denial. But she had her answer ready for him now.

'You told me,' she reminded him a trifle unsteadily, 'that you come from a religious family, that your upbringing was against immorality and promiscuity. Well, so was mine. I should have thought you of all people would be able to understand. It's not that I can't, but that I won't give in to you.'

'I also said,' his tone was taut with leashed passion, 'that the Trevelyans only made love to the women they intended to marry. I have asked you—a number of times—to marry me.'

Yes, she thought. But for the wrong reasons. She shook her head.

'The answer's still no, to marriage or to...to anything else.'

'My God!' It was a deep growl of frustration. 'If we were anywhere else but in the middle of a golf course I'd make you change your mind. I'd kiss you into submission, caress you until you begged me to make love to you.' His words, the tone in which they were uttered, were melting her bones. Her body throbbed with her need of him.

She mustered all her strength to answer him decidedly.

'And you might succeed. But afterwards you'd hate me and yourself. And I'd hate you, too. If I ever give myself to any man it will be because I want to, not because he forces or seduces me.'

'And you gave yourself to Tristram, but only for what you could get out of it! That isn't giving, Venna.'

Because she agreed with him, she had no answer, and he stood looking down at her for a long, charged moment. Then he turned on his heel and strode on ahead, so fast that she could not keep up with him.

At the clubhouse he handed in the borrowed clubs, and still in silence they walked back to where they had parked the car.

Keir slammed the passenger door and went round to the driver's side. He sat for some moments staring straight ahead of him. His fingers drummed an angry tattoo on the steering wheel. The tension seemed to fill the interior of the vehicle—a tangible, menacing thing. Apprehensively, Venna waited.

Gradually she sensed a change in the atmosphere, in Keir. The tension seemed to drain out of him. His hands relaxed and he turned towards her.

'All right, Venna,' he said tonelessly, 'I was out of order. You win—this time. But,' he went on, and now he spoke emphatically, 'if you do ever give yourself to a man, it's going to be me. Just remember that!'

'So, Venna! Where the hell have you been these last couple of weeks?'

Venna had insisted next morning that she must go into the shop to see Terry Little and try to come to some arrangement with him about dissolving their partnership. She wasn't looking forward to the interview, and she had scarcely set foot over the doorstep when he went into the attack. She'd had more than enough of angry men these last two days, she mused wryly.

'I've been stuck in this shop, unable to get out to any sales,' Terry went on. That was probably just as well, Venna thought.

'I left you a note explaining——' she began pacifyingly.

'Explaining nothing!' he retorted. 'All it told me was that you were going away for a few days and you didn't know when you'd be back.'

'I had some thinking to do.'

'And why do a moonlight like that?' he persisted. 'Why couldn't you have waited until the next morning and told me face to face? Instead of you "thinking", we might have been able to sort it out there and then. OK, so we had a row. Words were spoken that we probably both regret. But our engagement could have been on again within hours. Instead you...'

'I didn't go away to think about our engagement,' Venna interrupted him, and at his disconcerted expression, 'that's still off, Terry.' As he opened his mouth to protest, she went on, 'No, hear me out, please. If you're honest, you'll admit it would never have worked. We'd always be fighting.'

'It could have worked if it hadn't been for your half-sister's damned kid...'

'It wasn't just Gemma, Terry,' she told him. 'And you know it.' She'd intended to stay calm and rational. But now the old anger at his attitude towards her niece was coiling dangerously inside her. 'We were beginning to have other fundamental disagreements—about other things, and about business procedure in particular. I want to end our partnership. I'm...'

'Just like that!' He was scornful. 'Have you got someone willing to buy your share? Because I tell you, Venna, I can't afford to buy you out.' It was no more than she had suspected.

'I'm willing to give you a certain amount of time,' she conceded.

'Time! You know how slowly books turn over.'

'I'm willing to give you time,' she repeated. 'I'm going down to Cornwall for an unspecified period. I'm taking Gemma to meet her grandmother. While I'm away I want you to look around for another partner. And I'm going to have someone audit the accounts.' She thought Terry paled.

'Venna,' he almost pleaded, 'couldn't you rethink this? If I admit I was wrong? If I promise to treat the kid as if she were my own? There's no reason why we shouldn't go on as before.'

'Yes, there is, Terry. I'm sorry, but quite aside from our other disagreements I know now that I'm not in love with you. Perhaps I never was.'

'It's this Trevelyan fellow, isn't it?' he said with sudden angry suspicion. 'You've gone and fallen for him. Or you've made yourself believe you have, just because he's the kid's flesh and blood. You've been away with him, not on your own. My God, you're turning out just like that half-sister of yours. Well, don't come crawling back to me in a few months' time with *his* damned brat, and expect me to take the three of you in.'

Venna had struggled to keep her patience. She'd known Terry would be suffering from a sense of ill-usage. But she didn't honestly think she was to blame for anything more than leaving him short-staffed. It had been his fault she'd been driven into breaking off their engagement. Because of his recklessness in money matters they couldn't reconcile their business differences. Now, at his unpleasant insinuations, her fiery temper finally erupted.

'Don't worry!' she snapped. 'I wouldn't come to you for help if you were the last person on earth. And what's more, you can expect to hear from an auditor in the next couple of weeks, as soon as I can arrange it. And if the accounts are in the red, as I suspect they are, you'd better do something about it quickly, or you're liable to be prosecuted.' She turned on her heel and stalked towards the door.

'And will you really take action against him?' Keir asked curiously when a furious Venna related the details of her confrontation with Terry and her suspicions about the state of their joint finances. She omitted only Terry's unpleasant insinuations about her relationship with Keir.

'I'll have to,' she sighed. Her anger evaporated as suddenly as it had flared. 'I hate the idea. It seems so vindictive, especially after Terry and I had been so close.' She grimaced. 'But if I don't, it means I can write off my investment.'

'Can you afford to do that?'

'No,' she admitted.

'Leave it with me,' Keir said. 'I'll get my accountant on to it. It will make things less embarrassing for you.'

'You don't want to be bothered with my problems,' Venna protested. But it would be a relief, she thought, to have an impartial arbitrator. She didn't relish long-drawn-out haggling with Terry. Nor could she afford such a large loss. She would need her share of the money if she were to start up all over again.

'Leave it to me,' Keir repeated. 'By the way, the hospital phoned while you were out. They said...'

'Why on earth didn't you tell me before?' Venna demanded. 'Instead of letting me rabbit on about Terry? Is it...?'

'You didn't give me much chance,' he pointed out humorously.

But Venna's face had gone white with anxiety.

'Is Gemma...?'

'She's OK,' he reassured her. 'In fact, we can collect her tomorrow. Can you be ready to leave for London the day after?'

Gemma was still pale and not yet her usual lively self, but she withstood the long car journey well. Nevertheless, Venna was glad when they reached the city and Keir's flat. After depositing their luggage Keir had gone straight on to his office, leaving Venna to make lunch for herself and Gemma, and settle her niece down for an afternoon rest.

This done, she was rather at a loose end, which gave her time to examine and speculate on her surroundings.

She had been very much surprised to find that Keir's flat was in fact part of a converted warehouse complex in a very desirable area overlooking the River Thames. Apart from the situation, the conversion and the furnishings must have cost him a pretty penny, she thought. Unless of course the property was some kind of show-house which he was occupying until his estate agency sold it. She remembered reading somewhere that it was easier to sell property with the furnishings *in situ* than if it were standing empty.

Venna wandered curiously through a stainless-steel and marble bathroom, the sleek chrome, steel and marble kitchen, then back into the large room that did duty as living-room and dining-room.

Keir's décor wasn't to Venna's taste. It was sparse and understated. The furniture was all chrome and leather. No fabrics were used throughout the flat. Instead, all the windows had venetian blinds. The floors were of natural wood. And there was space—a lot of it in the linked L-shaped living-areas. Large black floor-cushions on thick-pile rugs made a comfortable place from which to watch television or listen to music.

Gemma was asleep in the bedroom she and Venna were to share, but Venna could not resist peeping into the master bedroom.

Here, too, black and grey predominated, with a splash of colour in the duvet and in a single modern painting that hung above the bed. Glass shelves held a few books, and Venna was drawn towards these as by a magnet. You could tell a lot about people, she contended, by their taste in reading.

But she was disappointed. These were all technical books, whereas her preference was for the arts. All in all, she decided, Keir's flat did nothing to further her knowledge of him. Except perhaps that he was a man who preferred to lead a simple, uncluttered life. It seemed that applied to his personal relationships too, since he had remained single all this time, untroubled by emotional entanglements.

She supposed Keir would be expecting her to prepare a meal for him. The refrigerator and deep-freeze were certainly well stocked. But, she realised, she had no idea when he would be home.

She was saved from further speculation by a telephone call around four o'clock from Keir's secretary,
who introduced herself simply as Sally. The message was
that they would be eating out.

'And he's roped me in to baby-sit,' Sally said. 'I'll be
over at six. Keir said you're to take a taxi and meet him
here at the office. He won't be through with his conference until about seven.'

Venna was uncertain about leaving Gemma with a
stranger. But then, she reassured herself, Sally *wasn't* a
stranger to Keir. And of one thing she was certain, Keir
had proved time and again that he had his niece's welfare
at heart. Suddenly she was looking forward to going out
with him.

But heavens, she only had two hours to get ready! It
didn't seem anywhere near long enough. Her nails needed
manicuring. Her hair needed washing. She had no idea
where Keir was taking her or what she should wear. She'd
brought a couple of evening dresses with her, but only
as a precaution. She hadn't really expected to need them.
And she hadn't unpacked. The dresses would be creased.

She tiptoed into the bedroom, where Gemma was still
asleep. The child looked very small in the large bed. She
still had an air of fragility, and Venna's soft heart
agonised as for a few moments she watched the sleeping
child. Gemma was so inexpressibly dear to her, and there
had been a few hours recently when Venna had thought
she was going to lose her.

At last, with a huge sigh, she recalled what she had
been about to do, and unpacked her suitcases.

The black dress, she decided critically. It wasn't new,
but it had been an expensive one. It looked good anywhere, and if she hung it in the bathroom while she
showered any creases would fall out.

The gleaming steel of the bathroom surfaces reflected
her slim, naked figure as effectively as any mirror. With
the discovery of her love for Keir had come a new

awareness of her body. Venna wasn't vain, but she caught herself trying to assess her appearance, as a man—as Keir—might see it.

Though she was petite, her slender legs were long in relation to her body. Her breasts were generously curved, but there wasn't an ounce of excess flesh on her hips and thighs, she thought, as she ran her hands over them. Her stomach was boyishly flat. Would anyone seeing her like this be able to tell that she'd never borne a child?

The thought sent her momentarily into a panic when she remembered that Keir *had* once seen her like this. But he couldn't have noticed anything, she reassured herself, or he would certainly have made some comment. She towelled briskly and went through to the bedroom to dress.

Gemma was awake and watched interestedly as Venna put on the black dress and skilfully applied make-up. The child accepted placidly the news that 'Auntie Sally' was coming to look after her. Venna thanked heaven her niece had never been difficult and clinging. Even so, when it was time to leave Venna carried a few anxieties with her.

Sally Harrison was older than she'd sounded on the phone. About thirty, Venna guessed, single and stunningly attractive. She seemed to know her way around the flat.

Venna wondered with a little stab of jealousy how often the other woman came there, and whether her relationship with Keir had always been purely that of employer and secretary. She hadn't realised before how painful loving could be. She'd never been jealous of any of her menfriends. Which only went to prove, she thought wryly, that she had never been properly in love before.

The taxi bore her swiftly through the teeming city streets to the address Sally had given her, an area Venna didn't know. She stared in disbelief when the vehicle stopped on the forecourt of an enormous modern tower block, and a uniformed commissionaire stepped forward to open the door.

She didn't know what she had expected, but it certainly hadn't been this massive complex, all of which appeared to be Pednolva Enterprises. Surely not?

But yes, Keir assured her when she was shown into his office, a room whose furnishings reflected those of the flat.

'When my grandfather, Nicholas Trevelyan, founded the firm, it was a relatively small enterprise. But old Nick—and yes, they did call him that to his face—was something of a financial wizard, and what began small soon increased in size. Under my father's management it expanded still further. And I like to think I've made my own modest contribution to expansion.'

Property-dealing was only one aspect of his business, Venna discovered. And she'd assumed he was just an estate agent! She blushed at the recollection. No wonder he'd seemed amused. Instead he was a property magnate, and quite likely a millionaire, too.

Pednolva Enterprises, he told her now, owned dozens of companies. And as they took his private lift to the ground floor he expounded to a still slightly disconcerted Venna his methods of import and export, manufacture and sales, and described an ever-growing number of factories and branch offices.

In his car on the way to the restaurant Keir talked of a world she had only heard of, a world of shareholders, of competition with other national and international companies. It was a scene far removed from the more gentle, intellectual world of books.

The restaurant was small and exclusive, richly furnished and dimly lit. But not so dimly lit that Venna could not see Keir's expression when he helped her to remove her coat and took in her appearance.

The black dress, narrow as a liquorice stick, clung sinuously close to her slender body, suspended from creamy shoulders by gold chain shoulder-straps. The simple garment's only other adornment was a coquettish frill that flared out from one hip and swirled down to the hemline.

She had always known that the dress suited her, but the frank male approbation in Keir's eyes fluttered Venna's pulses, and she was glad that it was the waiter's impersonal hand which, in pulling out her chair, brushed against her bare arm.

She allowed Keir to order for them both—a fillet steak cooked in wine, served with button mushrooms and tiny onions, together with an appropriate red wine.

'I'll need to spend another day in the office,' he told her as they ate. 'Then I think I can safely claim to be free for a couple of weeks. Will you mind spending another day at the flat?'

'It's very comfortable,' Venna assured him. 'But it's a bit unusual, isn't it? Did you choose the decorations? Do you spend much time there?'

Keir grinned.

'It is a bit antiseptic, isn't it? It was designed by the same firm who did the office décor. As a bachelor-pad it's OK. Of course, if you were to decide to marry me you could have a free hand with it. Alter the lot, if you like.' He refilled her wineglass. 'But we've talked enough about the flat and the office. Let's talk about you—about us. In these next weeks I want to learn more about you, Venna. There must be a lot you haven't told me.'

If he only knew! She shook her head.

'Not really.'

'I can't believe that. Somehow I sense hidden depths in you.' His expression was quizzical. 'And before we're very much older, I mean to discover what they are.'

Seated only a hand's reach across the small table from him, it was difficult for Venna to tear her gaze from his face long enough to deal with the food on her plate. He affected her senses far more potently than the heady wine they were drinking.

Keir, too, seemed more intent upon studying her than on eating. At times the expression in his grey eyes had all the tactile sensuality of a kiss. There was an intense awareness between them that the intimate atmosphere of the restaurant only served to promote. As his eyes roamed her face and neck, down over bare creamy shoulders to where the neckline of her dress revealed the swell of her breasts, Venna knew she had never been more aware of a man's masculinity or the fact that she was all female. With an odd tingling deep inside her that was almost like pain, she watched his long-fingered hands as they wielded the knife and fork, and imagined their touch on her body.

'Have you telephoned your mother yet?' she asked when she could bear this silent scrutiny no longer. She was feeling decidedly nervous about the coming encounter.

'No. I'll do that tonight when we get back to the flat.'

'What's she like?' Venna had meant in character, but immediately Keir took out his wallet from an inside pocket. He drew out a handful of photographs and passed them across the table. There were no single portraits, only groups of people.

Mrs Trevelyan was a tall, imposing woman, rather generously built, Venna thought, though it was hard to tell in view of the flowing draperies she wore in all the photos.

'That's my late sister,' Keir pointed a lean finger. 'The one Gemma takes after. That's my cousin—"young Nick". He runs our office in Japan.'

'And this?' Venna asked.

There was an odd little silence, then in a strange tone of voice Keir said, 'That's Tris.'

Despite the warmth of the restaurant, Venna went cold from head to foot. With family photographs she should have expected this, should have been on her guard against such a stupid blunder. But for a moment she had forgotten the role she was playing.

'Oh . . . of course.' She gave a nervous laugh. 'How silly of me. It must be this dim light . . . or perhaps it's a bad photograph,' she rambled on, miserably aware that she was only making things worse. Naturally Keir would be appalled that she hadn't recognised Gemma's father. He must think her totally callous and uncaring.

'It's quite a good likeness, actually,' Keir said as he retrieved the snaps and put them away. His voice was cold and remote. She couldn't think of anything to say to break the awkward moment, and she was relieved when Keir himself changed the subject. 'Something I have done today is to speak to my accounts department,' he told her. 'They'll be sending someone up to Southport the week after next to see your ex-partner.'

Venna murmured her thanks.

Over coffee, Keir asked her if she would like to go on somewhere to dance. Her insides quivered at the thought of this chance to be held in his arms. But she shook her head. He was probably only being polite. Besides, she told him, 'I'm sure your secretary's very efficient, but I don't want to be away from Gemma too long.'

The city streets were quieter as they drove back to the flat. Keir made no attempt at conversation, and Venna decided sadly that her failure to recognise his brother had probably served to worsen his opinion of her.

An electronic beam opened the garage doors. And as the car glided into the dark interior the doors closed again behind them.

It took Venna's eyes a second or two to adjust to the gloom. But when she moved to open the car door, Keir's hand on her arm restrained her.

'Wait,' he said huskily. 'I don't believe I told you how very lovely you looked tonight.' The words were a simple enough compliment, one she had received many times before. But she had never been so strongly affected. But then, it wasn't the compliment itself but the man who uttered it, the tone in which it was delivered.

In the still darkness of the car, Keir's voice throbbed strangely. The hand that had restrained her took her chin in a firm but gentle grip, turning her head towards him.

Painfully conscious of his nearness, her insides contracted sharply. She felt herself engulfed in the composite smell of his maleness. She could have freed herself from thrall, but she didn't. Instead, held in sensuous captivity, she found herself swaying towards him. Her breathing was suddenly shallow and erratic.

There was a moment of intensity before he pulled her, almost roughly, into his arms. He said her name fiercely. Then he was kissing her with a stinging passion and his hands were inside her coat, moving the length of her body.

Her fingers went on their own voyage of exploration, around his neck, tangling in the thick, dark waves where they overhung the collar of his shirt. She passed her hands over the contours of his face, blindly learning its bone structure. Against her soft palms his jawline was sensuously rough.

She knew this ought not to be happening, but she did not resist as he slid the coat from her shoulders. The chain straps of her dress followed suit, so that he could uncover and caress her breasts. As his thumb brought their nubs to sensitive life, she croaked his name imploring, wanting, needing more.

Tremblingly she unbuttoned his shirt and slid her hands inside, over the rough hairs on his chest, around and down his back. He was silk and steel, and as she reached the base of his spine he shuddered and pulled her against him with such ferocity that she gave a little cry of pain.

Where his fingers touched her, flames seemed to lick her flesh. She trembled against him, her heart pounding against her ribs as she returned kiss for kiss. Desire rose ever higher within her, and she knew he was similarly affected, that their embrace was reaching a dangerous ardour.

'Venna! Oh, God, Venna!' His voice was thick with need. 'Your body's so beautiful.' His mouth took possession of one nipple, tormenting it deliciously. 'I haven't been able to think about anything else all evening. Tell me,' he asked throatily, 'did you wear this dress for deliberate effect?'

She tensed slightly as he pushed her skirt upwards, exposing her thighs, but his mouth stifled her protest, and then as his hands continued their exploration she was beyond protesting, and as they reached their destination she groaned harshly, her hips moving in an involuntary, convulsive invitation.

'You want me!' he said positively. 'You're ready for me *now*. Admit it, Venna.'

He was right, damn him. She ought to deny it, as she ought to deny the intimacies his hands were seeking, but she couldn't. Just as she was wondering what she would do if he really attempted to make love to her here in his car, he released her, even more abruptly than he had taken her into his arms. He reached up and flicked on the interior light. He stared at her, his grey eyes dilated, and she saw that anger warred with desire in them.

'Was it like that with Tris, Venna?' he demanded harshly. 'Was it? I have to know.'

She looked wonderingly at him, so that there was no need for him to say, as he did, harshly, 'Look at me, Venna!' Then, 'Go on! Take a good, long look, so that you'll know me again. Because I'm going to make damned sure that you never forget what *I* look like!'

CHAPTER EIGHT

FOR a split second Venna stared at Keir disbelievingly, her green eyes huge with pain. At first she was unable to credit what her ears told her. Then sudden nausea assailed her as she realised just what he had done to her and why.

Tears stinging behind her eyes, she fumbled blindly for the door-handle. She found it, scrambled from the car, then stumbled towards the door that connected with the main building. It was a heavy fire door, and it took her a moment or two to grapple with it.

Vaguely, somewhere behind her, she heard the slamming of the car doors and knew Keir was following her. The knowledge made her increase her stumbling pace. But she wasn't fast enough. As she mounted the first flight of stairs, she heard Keir's uneven footsteps ringing on the concrete surfaces behind her.

It was impossible to outdistance him, even if her legs hadn't been trembling so much. Besides, she had no key to the flat. She could only wait, sick and shivering, for him to let her in.

She didn't look at him as he came up with her.

'Venna——' he began.

'Don't speak to me!' she told him, her voice taut with the effort of controlling the nausea.

'Venna! Listen to me!' The command echoed hollowly around the landing.

'I don't want to hear any more.' She didn't realise her voice was rising, pitched dangerously near to hysteria. 'You've said enough. But I'm not what you...'

'Keir! I thought I heard your voice! Thank God!' Sally Harrison threw open the door. Her tone was one of utter relief. Her *soignée* appearance had been considerably impaired by the agitation she displayed.

At once Venna's intuition told her the cause of the other woman's disturbed manner.

'What is it?' Her voice was still shrill, but with apprehension now. 'It's Gemma, isn't it?' Without waiting for a reply she pushed past the other woman and ran into the flat, into the bedroom. The bed was tumbled but empty. There was no sign of Gemma. She rushed back to where Sally was now confronting Keir.

'You might have warned me I'd be looking after a *sick* child. I had no idea where to contact you. I've been worried out of my mind.'

'Where is she?' Venna demanded. 'Where's Gemma? What have you done with her?'

'I had to call an ambulance. They've taken her to hospital.'

Nausea had continued to threaten Venna ever since she had realised Keir's deliberate intent to punish her. Now it erupted and, a hand clapped over her mouth, she bolted for the bathroom. She regurgitated the contents of her meal abruptly and painfully. She clung to the cold steel surfaces as she retched in violent spasms.

Strong hands supported her against the unpleasant contractions. A deep voice murmured words of consolation and encouragement.

'Take it steady now, Venna. Don't immediately assume the worst. Look, I'll go straight round to the hospital.'

'No! I'll go!' She found sufficient strength to choke out the words, for she was crying now. 'On my own. I don't need you!'

'You may think that right at this moment. But nevertheless——' Firmly he sat her down on the edge of the bath and sponged her flushed face. He proffered a handkerchief and with brusque practicality made up a mouthwash. 'Use this, then we'll get going.'

Her brief spurt of defiance was at an end. She obeyed. At this moment Gemma's health and safety were more important than her feud with Keir. Besides, it was her own fault Keir thought she was the woman Tristram had loved. His treatment of her had been the outcome of her failure to recognise the photograph of his brother. Gemma's real mother *would* have recognised him. She was lucky that Keir was only angry, and not suspicious.

She was shivering now.

'Change into something warmer,' Keir ordered. 'We may be in for a long wait at the hospital.'

'There isn't time...'

'Yes, there is. By the time you've pulled on slacks and a sweater I'll have the car out again and round at the front. Now get on with it.'

If she'd been the woman he thought her, the self-sufficient, man-scornful Shelagh, she would have resented Keir's high-handedness. Venna wasn't the helpless type, by any means, but it was comforting, as it had been when Gemma was first taken ill, to have his strength and matter-of-fact calm to support her, to have someone tell her exactly what to do.

Fortunately it was no great distance to the hospital. Even so, Venna sat tensely upright in the passenger seat as she willed the car to go faster, as she fretted at every red light.

'If only we hadn't gone out,' she said at one point. 'I'll never forgive myself for not being there.'

'I know and I'm sorry, my dear. But even if we *had* been there, we couldn't have stopped Gemma being ill,' Keir added practically. 'And Venna,' briefly he put one hand on her knee, 'I'm sorry too...about... If I'd known what we were going to find when we got back, I'd never have...'

'Forget it,' she said brusquely. 'It's not important.'
And it wasn't. At least, not at the moment. She knew
that later the pain of it would recur, but she was too
numb with fear now to feel anything else.

'I see!' he said curtly. 'Well, in that case...' He did
not finish his sentence, but she had the impression that
despite his words he was still angry with her.

Except for the fact that it was a different hospital, as
its antiseptic atmosphere engulfed her, Venna felt as
though she were reliving the earlier nightmare.

Gemma had been put through the same rigorous tests
as before, with the same result. Her other kidney had
seized up. Another operation was about to take place.

It had been a long day. In fact, it seemed as though
more than a day had passed since they had left Southport
early that morning. Both Keir and Venna were tired. They
sat side by side in the waiting-room, neither of them
speaking. It had been so different the last time, Venna
thought unhappily. She'd been able to pour out all her
fears and Keir had done much to counter them. This
time there seemed to be an insuperable barrier between
them. From time to time she ventured to look at him,
and on a couple of occasions saw his head nod in sleep.

In all honesty, she couldn't blame him. She knew it
wasn't lack of concern on his part. As well as the long
drive, he'd had a busy afternoon and evening at the
office, and it had been well after midnight when they
had returned to the flat. If she felt weary and emotionally
drained, so must he. But Venna could not sleep.

It was five o'clock in the morning when the urologist
himself came to tell them Gemma had come safely
through the operation.

'It's a pity, though, that we didn't know the child's
medical history when she was admitted,' he pointed out.
'It might have saved time.'

'I blame myself for that,' Keir told Venna. 'But it never
occurred to me to tell Sally about Gemma's previous op-

eration.' His face was grey with fatigue, his eyes shadowed, making him look a decade older than his thirty-nine years.

'It's not your fault,' she said generously. 'We neither of us had any reason to think her illness would flare up again.'

His expression did not lighten, but he reached for her hand and grasped it tightly. She returned the pressure, the comforter for once.

They were allowed to see Gemma briefly. Again there were the pipes and tubes. After one look at her baby niece, Venna turned her face against Keir's shoulder. She shook with silent sobs.

He held her close until the paroxysms subsided. Then gently he steered her towards the door.

At this she resisted.

'I'm staying!'

'Not this time!' he said firmly. 'This time you're not going to get overtired and run down. This time I'm here to look after you. This is probably the best hospital in the country. Gemma will receive every care and attention.'

Though she would never have believed it possible, Venna fell into an exhausted sleep in the car on the return journey, and Keir had to wake her. Still half-drunk with sleep, she allowed him to support her up the stairs and into the flat.

'You'd better go straight to bed,' he told her, and she nodded submissively. 'Get undressed and I'll bring you in a hot drink. Do you need anything to make you sleep?'

She shook her head. She didn't like taking tablets unless absolutely necessary.

She was so tired, she shed her clothes in a heap at the foot of the bed, and she was already dozing when Keir came in with a glass of hot milk. He sat on the edge of the bed and watched her drink it. He looked dreadfully tired himself, she thought, with a painful twist of her heart.

'Go to bed,' she told him. 'You need to rest, too.'

'Yes,' he agreed, but he made no move to leave. Then, 'Venna, we have to talk, about what happened tonight— last night, I should say.'

She didn't pretend not to understand.

'Please, Keir,' she begged wearily, 'not now. I know what you think of me, why you did what you did. But I don't think I can take any more.' Her voice trembled. 'Not on top of Gemma being ill.' She gazed pleadingly at him through tear-hazed eyes, and he swore softly.

'My God, Venna! What kind of brute do you take me for?' His broad shoulders sagged and he buried his head in his hands, running them ferociously through his hair until it stood out as roughly as a terrier's coat. 'Well, I suppose I can't blame you. But I'm not looking for a confrontation, my dear. All I want is for us to establish some kind of truce if we can.' He raised his head and looked at her earnestly. 'Do you think that's possible?'

'I've never wanted us to be at loggerheads,' Venna told him with quiet truth.

'You see,' he went on almost as if he hadn't heard her, his hands busy again dishevelling his hair, 'I find myself in a totally baffling situation where you're concerned. There are so many inconsistencies—in your character, in your behaviour. All the time I was searching for you I had this picture of a hard-faced, hard-hearted harpy. I was ready to hate you. And God knows I've tried to feed that hatred.' He sounded bewildered. 'But I haven't succeeded. I can't hate you, Venna. But I've made *you* hate *me*,' he concluded wearily. 'Haven't I?'

'No,' she sighed. 'I don't hate you.' She wanted to put her arms about his bowed shoulders and smooth his ruffled hair, but she dared not. 'I understand how you feel about me.'

'Do you?' He looked up again, his expression a strange one. 'I doubt it. Oh, I doubt it very much.'

But she nodded vehemently, intent on convincing him.

'Of course I understand. I know how you must feel about your brother. I would have felt exactly the same about anyone who'd hurt my sister—my half-sister.'

'Oh! I see!' There was a kind of tired amusement in his voice. He was silent for a moment. 'You were very close, you and your half-sister? Isn't that unusual?'

'Maybe. I don't know. But yes, we were extremely fond of each other. I'd have done anything for Shelagh, and she for me.'

Keir stood up. But he remained by the bed, looking down at her.

'So you don't hate me?'

She shook her head.

'And we do have a truce? Of a kind?'

'Yes.' Shyly she held out her hand. 'We can shake on it, if you like.'

He looked at the hand she had extended towards him, and for an instant she thought he wasn't going to take it. But then his fingers closed over it, his grip almost painful. But he didn't shake her hand, nor did he release it.

'Just one more thing, Venna. Then I'll leave you to get some rest. What I'm going to say, please don't reject it out of hand. Think about it, for as long as you like. I'm prepared to wait.'

She knew what was coming, and she tried to withdraw her hand, but he wouldn't let her.

'Keir...' she began nervously.

'No, hear me out. I want you to think again about marrying me. As I said before, I'm not asking for love. I know that's impossible.' Venna winced, but she managed to keep the pain out of her face. 'But you and Gemma do need someone to take care of you. These last few weeks have proved that beyond a shadow of doubt.

Let me take care of you both, Venna, please. Marry me.'
And, as she parted her lips in another attempt at protest,
he continued 'I won't give you any cause to regret it.
You can have as much freedom within the marriage as
you want. I'll be there in times of trouble—though God
knows, I hope there won't be any more trouble. And
besides, I need an heir!'

At this, Venna shuddered and the sensation made itself
felt to him through the communication of their hands.
His grip tightened.

'I should have said heiress,' he said harshly. 'Naturally I was referring to Gemma. I'm not asking you to
share my bed.' He released her hand, and this time he
did move towards the door. 'Think about it, Venna. After
all, can you really square it with your conscience to deny
Gemma the security I can give her?' Drily, 'As you know,
I'm not exactly poverty-stricken.'

Well, he had successfully destroyed all chance of her
getting any sleep, Venna thought as the door closed
behind him. Now her brain must worry away at this new
problem, one she had believed to be already resolved.

Keir had a point. Since he had no children, Gemma
would be a considerable heiress some day. It would be
unfair to deny the child the advantages that promised.
Venna did battle with her conscience. If Keir only knew
it, he didn't have to marry her to achieve his object. She
was a bit hazy about the legalities, but she believed he
had more right to Gemma than she did.

But if she owned up, she would lose Gemma. Not only
that. She could also say goodbye to Keir Trevelyan. Both
notions were totally unacceptable. So, an insidious inner
voice demanded, why not marry him? On this thought,
oddly enough, she fell asleep.

During the next few days they spent many hours at the
hospital, and Venna became increasingly anxious.
Gemma was taking longer to rally this time. The child

had lost a lot of weight, and looked pale and thin. She couldn't eat, and was being force-fed through a nasal gastric tube.

'I don't think I can stand much more of this,' Venna told Keir after one visit to the hospital. 'She doesn't seem to be making any progress. I'm so afraid she's not going to get better this time.'

'She will!' he told her, a hand on her shoulder. 'Gemma's got a good constitution. You must have given her a very good start in life.' The pressure of his hand increased. 'You're a good mother, Venna.' Then, a little hesitantly, 'Have you thought any more about marrying me? I know you've had other things on your mind but...'

'Yes, I've thought about it,' Venna said quietly. 'Quite a lot, actually.'

'And?' Through the grip of his hand, she sensed his tension.

'I've . . . I've even tried praying,' she went on, feeling a little embarrassed by the admission, 'though I'm not sure I really believe in it. I just wish there was some kind of answer, so that I knew someone was listening.' She hesitated at what she was going to say next, then, 'Do you . . . do you think God makes bargains?'

'What kind of bargains?' She'd expected him to laugh at her, but he was quite serious.

She didn't know how to go on. Then she summoned up all her courage, drew a deep breath, and, not looking at him, said, 'I . . . I promised your God that if he made Gemma better, I'd . . . I'd marry you!' She said the last three words in a hurried, breathless rush, then waited anxiously for some reaction. She didn't know what she had expected. Certainly not rapture. But she was a little taken aback by his matter-of-fact response.

'Good!' he said briskly. 'In that case, I'll see about getting a licence.'

She wished she could feel as certain as he seemed to be about Gemma's eventual recovery. She also felt a little stunned. She had made a decision, given a promise that might be impossible to revoke. The strictures of her grandmother and the nuns had made a strong impression on her. And, even though she wasn't sure she believed in God, she had a superstitious dread that Gemma's life did indeed hang on the faithful performance of her promise.

A week later there was no doubt that the child was on the mend. And a fortnight later Venna married Keir Trevelyan in a quiet church service with only two witnesses present—Sally Harrison and another woman from his office.

Romantically inclined, Venna had always dreamed of a white wedding followed by a honeymoon in some exotic, out-of-the way place. But this was reality. There was no need for a honeymoon when your husband wasn't in love with you.

Sally Harrison didn't seem surprised when she was told they weren't going away, Venna thought. Perhaps, as Keir's personal secretary, she even knew the truth about their marriage. Venna found herself strongly resenting the notion. But she welcomed the presence of the two women at a simple restaurant meal after the ceremony. She was aware of a new awkwardness now that she and Keir were actually married. Although for the past fortnight they had both occupied the flat without anyone else present, she found herself dreading going back there and being alone with him now they were man and wife. It wasn't going to make any difference to their relationship, she kept reminding herself. But somehow that was no consolation at all.

'It'll be another two weeks at least before we can even think of going down to Cornwall,' Keir told her as he unlocked what was now their door and she preceded him into the flat's small hallway. 'So I may as well put in some time at the office. You won't mind being alone here all day?'

'No, of course not.' It was the sensible thing for him to do, but she was aware of disappointment.

'Do you know London at all? There's plenty to see. Historic buildings, museums, art galleries. Then there's always the shops. I've opened an account in your name at my bank. Eventually we'll bring the rest of your things down from Southport, but until then why not treat yourself to a whole new wardrobe?' Wryly, 'One of us might as well derive something from this marriage.'

At once Venna was determined she wouldn't spend a penny of his money on herself. But she wasn't going to tell him so. His obvious meaning, that he expected no pleasure at all from their marriage, was not unexpected. But it hurt all the same.

Her tone was sharp with pain as she asked, 'Have you told your mother about us?'

'Not yet.'

'Putting off the evil moment?' she taunted out of her anguish.

'Something like that,' he agreed.

For the next few days her life followed a regular pattern. She got up, made Keir's breakfast, saw him off to the office like a dutiful wife, occupied his absence with housework and cooked him a meal for when he returned. But there any semblance of normality ended.

She spent as much time as possible at the hospital. When Keir had no business engagements in the evening he went out with her. Then when they returned to the flat their lives diverged once more. He often brought paperwork home which, apparently, engrossed him to the exclusion of everything else.

Venna supposed she could have sat with him in the living-room while he worked. But she couldn't very well watch television, and for the first time in her life she found herself totally unable to concentrate on a book. She tried, but she could not keep her eyes on the printed page. Instead, time and time again she found they had strayed to her husband. Her husband! How strange that sounded. It sounded unreal. Was unreal.

Even so, she hungrily devoured the lineaments of his face till she knew every feature by heart, knew the way the crisp hair curled on his neck. With her eyes shut she could see the muscular breadth of his back and shoulders, could visualise the long, slightly spatulate fingers that could grip so strongly but could caress so subtly, arouse so insidiously.

She found herself studying the way his clothes outlined his body, obsessed with imaginings of how he would look without them. There was sheer physical torture in such speculations which finally drove her from the room to seek her bed. And even there she lay awake long after she'd heard him go to his own room, wishing, longing for him to come to her and satisfy the sexual cravings just the sight and thought of him aroused in her.

She tried not to let these frustrations show in her manner towards him, but she knew there were times when her voice sounded unnecessarily sharp, just as at times he spoke harshly to her. It was all very well for him to say he had found himself unable to hate her. But if it wasn't hatred, it was something very akin to it. It was an impossible situation, yet they had bound themselves to it for a lifetime. Keir's strong beliefs, she knew, made divorce out of the question.

'I'm going away for a few days,' he told her totally out of the blue one morning.

Until then she hadn't noticed the suitcase standing on the floor beside his usual briefcase.

'Where to? For how long?' she asked, then bit her lip. She hadn't the rights of a normal wife to question his comings and goings.

He obviously thought so too, for all he said was, 'It's a business trip. I don't know how long it will take.'

'I see!' Venna pushed aside her untasted breakfast. He might not come back... Of course he would. If not for her, then he would be back for Gemma.

As usual, she saw him to the door. He probably couldn't care less whether she did or not. But at least for those few minutes it gave her the illusion, about the only one she had, that theirs was a normal marriage.

Usually he bade her a formal goodbye and departed without even turning back to look at her. This morning he paused in the hall.

'If you need me urgently, Sally knows where to contact me.' He could tell Sally, but he wouldn't tell his wife, Venna thought resentfully. 'If they say Gemma can come home before I get back, take good care of her and...and of yourself.' He hesitated, still looking down at her. There was something brooding in the atmosphere, and for a moment Venna could almost fancy he was about to kiss her goodbye. But it must have been wishful thinking on her part, for the moment passed and, with his usual brief nod, he was gone.

Well, she wasn't going to pine, Venna decided as she brushed away a few tears. He wouldn't miss her, and when he came back she certainly wasn't going to look as if *she'd* missed *him*.

When she wasn't visiting Gemma, she was going to do what he had initially suggested. She was going to shop for new clothes. And she was going to explore London. She would eat all her meals out and the housework could go hang! All she had been these last few days was a glorified housekeeper anyway. In fact, when Keir came back she was going to tell him he could employ some domestic help. When Gemma was quite recovered, she, Venna, was going to find work of some kind. She might even take a trip back to Southport and see if Terry had found himself a new partner. It was unhealthy all those empty hours she had spent lately, aching for things she couldn't have.

It wasn't easy to keep her resolution. Once upon a time she would have enjoyed exploring London, even on her own. But as she studied famous paintings in the National Gallery and marvelled at the Crown jewels in the Tower, she kept wanting to turn to Keir and share her pleasure with him.

Even second-hand bookshops seemed to have lost their usual magical allure. Once she could have spent contented hours browsing among their shelves, to emerge dusty but happy with some long-looked-for treasure of literature.

But doggedly she stuck at it. And every day Gemma improved. Another two or three days, the doctors thought, and Venna would be able to take her home. There was no reason either, with care, they said, why the child should not be taken down to Cornwall.

Altogether Keir had been away five days when Venna heard the sound for which her ears had been continually alert, the sound of his latch-key in the lock. But she forced herself to remain seated. Even when she heard him throw down his case and briefcase with what seemed unnecessary violence, she kept her eyes on the book she had been attempting to read, and only looked up with forced nonchalance when he was actually standing over her.

Then the book fell from a hand made suddenly nerveless by the expression in his eyes.

CHAPTER NINE

FOR an instant Venna could have sworn she had seen tenderness in his face. But the fleeting impression must have been the product of her imagination, the fevered response of her senses to his presence. For in the next moment she saw that his face wore its most guarded, unfathomable expression.

He picked up the book and looked at the title before returning it to her.

'H-how was your trip?' was all she could think of to say. She forced herself not to look directly at him again, though she burned to devour his familiar face feature by feature. She had missed him so much.

'*Most* satisfactory!' It was not just a polite rejoinder to her question. His tone was one of genuine complacency and Venna waited for him to enlarge on the subject. But perhaps he thought she wouldn't be interested in business, for instead he asked, 'How's Gemma?'

'Fine!' At once Venna's face glowed and she looked up at him, all self-consciousness forgotten. 'She came home yesterday. She's in bed, asleep.'

His grey eyes lit up and he moved towards the bedroom door, then hesitated.

'May I?'

'Yes, of course. You won't disturb her. She's always been a sound sleeper.' Drawn by an impulse she couldn't resist, Venna stood up and followed him.

Side by side they stood looking down at the sleeping child. Venna stole a hungry sideways glance at Keir's swarthy features, and saw them suffused by an affection she coveted for herself.

'It's good to see her looking well again,' he said softly.

As they left the bedroom, Keir put an arm about Venna's shoulders and turned her towards him. His arm was heavy, warm through the material of her blouse. Tremulously she looked up at him, wondering what his actions portended. His eyes were searching her face.

'And you don't regret your bargain?' he asked.

He didn't have to explain. Venna coloured slightly as she shook her head. Then she mustered her courage.

'Why? Do you?' she asked, and found the temerity to hold his gaze.

He didn't answer immediately, and as she stared at his inscrutable expression she began to wish she hadn't asked. Then, slowly, his face relaxed into lines of amusement.

'Oh, no, Venna! Far from it! I find myself increasingly satisfied with the bargain *I* made.' Now what exactly did *that* mean? she wondered a trifle crossly. But evidently he wasn't about to satisfy her curiosity, for he went on, 'Is there any reason why we shouldn't leave for Cornwall tomorrow morning?'

'None that I can think of,' she admitted reluctantly. Now the visit was imminent, she wished there were some way the ordeal could be delayed.

'Good!' he said briskly. 'In that case, I'll telephone my mother.' He went into his bedroom and Venna heard the click as he picked up the extension.

The deep rumble of his voice went on for some considerable time, and Venna wondered what on earth he was finding to talk about. But she supposed his sudden marriage would take some explaining.

Once, she even heard him laugh. It was an attractive sound, one of genuine mirth. She relaxed a little. Surely he wouldn't be laughing if his mother had taken exception to his news? All the same, she wished she knew exactly what he was telling Mrs Trevelyan about her.

She was just thinking she might as well go to bed, in case Keir wanted an early start next morning, when he emerged from his room.

'That's settled, then!' He still wore his expression of amused satisfaction. But he raised his eyebrows at seeing her half-way to her bedroom door. 'Not off yet, are you? I was hoping you might join me in a coffee.' Since he immediately sat down in one of the black leather chairs, it was obvious he had no intention of making it himself. But Venna was so pleased to have him back, she had no objections to waiting on him.

'In other words,' she said with wry humour, 'you'd like *me* to make one for you?'

He responded to her smile with a deprecatory one of his own.

'And a few sandwiches, perhaps? Would you mind? It's been a long day and a long drive.'

She waited. Perhaps now he would enlighten her further about his whereabouts during the past few days. But as nothing more was forthcoming she went into the kitchen.

To her surprise, after a moment or two, he followed her. He leaned on the worktop, watching her every move. The kitchen was a reasonable size, but immediately it seemed smaller and Venna felt confined and self-conscious.

'I thought you were tired,' she said at last, when she could bear that intent, silver-grey scrutiny no longer.

'Mmmn-hm!' It was an untranslatable grunt.

'I don't need any help, you know,' she told him with a touch of desperation when his gaze remained as rigidly fixed. She was aware of the tell-tale pulse that flickered in her neck, and hoped he hadn't observed it.

Again that unintelligible sound.

'Why don't you go and sit down if you're tired?' she demanded, an edge of exasperation creeping into her tone. 'I'll bring these through when they're ready.'

'I like watching you,' he said simply.

'Oh!' The knife Venna was using slipped off the edge of the ham she was slicing and clattered to the floor.

He moved towards her. He bent down and picked up the knife. She held out her hand for it, but he put it out of reach on the worktop and took her hand in his.

'You seem unusually nervous tonight, Venna? Why's that?'

'Nervous? Me? No!' She attempted a laugh, but it came out false and high-pitched. 'Why should I be nervous?'

'That's what I'm asking myself.' Absently, it seemed, he was caressing the palm of her hand. 'Is it the thought of meeting my mother?'

She *was* dreading it. But that was tomorrow. This was here and now. She swallowed to clear the obstruction in her throat and passed her tongue over lips that felt suddenly dry. His fascinated gaze watched her mouth.

'Or is it something to do with me?' He had hold of both her hands now, and she had the strangest sensation that the steely walls of the room were coming closer. Then she realised with a sharp thrill of horror that it was she who had moved. She had swayed towards him. For a few seconds she had actually felt her whole body reach out for him.

'N-no,' she lied. She tried to jerk away, but he drew her towards him.

'I think it has a lot to do with me,' he told her.

'No! It hasn't. Please ... let me go. The coffee! Your sandwiches!' she said incoherently.

'Forget them for the moment. There's something else I need more urgently.' Above the grey eyes the lids were hooded, sleepily sensual.

'Keir!' She guessed his intention a split second before it happened. 'No!' She was terrified of what might happen if he kissed her, of what it might lead to.

'Yes, Venna! Oh, yes!' he murmured thickly against her lips. 'After all, what's a kiss between husband and wife?'

She struggled and managed to free her mouth long enough to protest.

'This wasn't part of our bargain!'

'No,' he agreed, but he didn't sound in the least penitent. 'But I don't see why we can't extend our bargain to include it. Do you?'

'No. I mean, no, we can't...I can't...' But he was pressing little feathery kisses along the side of her jaw, down the column of her throat where that betraying pulse still fluttered like a trapped creature.

'Relax, Venna!' His hand had found the curve of her breast, the appeal of its full roundness emphasised by the soft fabric of the blouse she wore. His touch was arousing remembered sensations. And as he pulled her hard against the taut muscularity of his body the knowledge of his arousal sent answering tremors through her. She yielded with a sudden sigh, her mouth seeking his, as she let his hands and lips have their will of her.

'That's better!' He had kissed her before, but surely never with this sensual power? This kiss held a different quality from his earlier ones. His mouth was as demanding, as possessive, yet it was tender and she responded with an intensity that matched his.

As the fervour of their kisses increased they were both breathing raggedly, their bodies entwined, straining together as though they could never be close enough to each other. His hands moved over her in passionate, seeking caresses. Slowly but surely he was edging her out of the kitchen, moving towards his bedroom door.

'I want you, Venna,' he told her huskily. 'Now!'

'Keir, you promised. You said a marriage in name only.' But she knew her voice carried no conviction.

'And what if I find I can't keep that promise? That I no longer want to? Will you still hold me to it? Even though you want me as much as I want you?' He didn't wait for her answer, but went on, his eyes searching the face he would not allow her to hide from him, 'When I made you that promise it was under different circumstances. Things have changed.'

Venna shook her head in bewilderment. What had changed? Nothing, so far as she was concerned.

'Yes,' he insisted, 'I know you a lot better now, my darling. You're in my blood. From the first moment I saw you I knew you were a woman I'd want to possess. But I never guessed just how much that need would take hold of me. Perhaps it was just as well. If I had guessed I might have gone away and never known...'

'You wanted me?' Venna asked incredulously. 'Even though you hated and despised me, because of your brother? No, Keir,' she shook her head, 'I don't believe you. You're up to your old tricks. Do you think I've forgotten the last time? You're not going to punish me again for something I...'

'Don't worry, my darling.' His hold on her tightened so that she could feel the swelling need of his hard, strong body. 'You won't find this any punishment. Quite the contrary.' He bent his head, and despite her attempt at evasion his lips were on hers again, firm but coaxing, destroying her resistance. Again he was urging her, step by step, towards the bedroom door.

She was on fire for him. She ached to be possessed. Why not? her anguished flesh cried out. Why not? After all, they were married now.

His breathing quickened as he felt all the fight drain out of her. With a little cry of triumph he lifted her in his arms and strode the remaining distance. Inside, he leant against the door to close it. Then he was lowering her on to his bed and he was on top of her, his body an exquisite weight, crushing her into the mattress, his kisses growing deeper and ever more demanding.

Their hearts thudded in unison and Venna's hands curled about his neck as he murmured, 'I want you as I've never wanted any other woman in my life.'

She felt the fastening of her skirt give way to his importunate hands. He dealt as easily with the buttons of her blouse, the clip of her bra, and she felt him shudder convulsively as his lips sought her breasts and their rosy areola that had peaked to his lovemaking.

She began to explore his body as he was exploring hers, thrilling to its muscularity. His skin was damp with perspiration, and she knew from his taut erectness that it would not be long now before he took her. She wanted him too, but she must warn him, before it was too late, not to hurt her.

Not to hurt her! Suddenly Venna went rigid. How could she have allowed herself to be so carried away as to forget? The remembrance of her virginity brought her back to sanity with a painful thump, and the dreadful realisation that if Keir made love to her he would know! He would know that she'd never made love before in her life. He would know she couldn't be Gemma's mother. The thought of his anger when he discovered how she had deceived him was an effectual turn-off.

Panic-stricken, she began to fight him, pushing against his broad shoulders with all the strength she could muster.

'Now what? Venna! You can't deny me now!' His voice was harsh with unslaked desire. 'For God's sake, woman, why—when you know you want me?'

'Yes, I *can* deny you! I'm doing so.' Though she too burned with unsatisfied yearning, she continued to struggle. 'Let go of me, Keir. I don't want you.'

'Liar!' He was still trying to restrain her, his lips and hands still attempted to coax her back into submission. But fear of discovery had lent her strength and resolution. 'Why, Venna?' he demanded again. He had suc-

ceeded in pinning her to the bed, but now she sensed
that the urgency had gone out of his body. 'Tell me.'

'No!' she retorted. 'Just leave me alone.'

'Is it because you're afraid I'll . . . ?'

'I'm not afraid,' she said mendaciously. 'I just want
you to stick to the terms of our bargain, a marriage of
convenience, you said. Well, don't expect me to agree
to anything else. With no love on either side what you're
doing is . . . is lust.'

At this, he did release her.

'I see!' She hated the cynical twist to his mouth.
'Perhaps so. But do you think we're going to be able to
live together, year after year, denying the impulses of
the flesh? It won't be easy, my dear. Because however
much you deny it, I know you want me as much as I
want you. You have all along.'

'No!'

'I don't believe that, Venna. Everything about you
when I make love to you tells a different story. Perhaps
one day you'll give me a more convincing explanation.
Perhaps one day you'll tell me the truth.' He sat back
on his heels and she rolled free of him.

With trembling hands she picked up her skirt and
fastened her blouse. His face was expressionless now.
She had expected anger. But he seemed drained of all
violent emotion. In fact, she could almost have imagined she saw wry amusement. At her expense, no
doubt. Trust Keir to find mirth in a situation like this.
The last thing she felt like was laughter.

Like Gemma, Venna dozed most of the way next day.
She'd had very little sleep the previous night. Her brain
had been as stimulated as her body and she'd gone over
in imagination not only every kiss, every caress, but every
word Keir had said. He had said that one day perhaps
she would tell him the truth. But then, the truth was far
from anything he could possibly conceive. She was re-

alistic enough to know she couldn't expect to get away
with her deception for the rest of their lives, that she
would have to tell him soon. But she dreaded the moment
of revelation. Keir would be justifiably angry, and she
couldn't begin to imagine what form his retribution
would take.

She was fully awake when they crossed the border into
Cornwall. As they neared their destination it was late
afternoon, but still light enough to see her surroundings.

They drove along delightful narrow lanes that could
hardly be dignified by the name of roads. A dip in the
high hedges or a twist in the lane frequently offered a
glimpse of sea or revealed a charming group of thatch-
roofed cottages. Under different circumstances Venna
would have been enjoying the scenic treat.

Gradually the landscape became bleaker, greyer, a
world of stark, rock-like shapes, savage, strong, primitive, yet strangely beautiful. And to one side of the road
there was the unending presence, the ceaseless breathing
of the sea.

A pair of impressive gates set in a grey wall and a
'Private' sign announced that they had reached their
destination. Within the walls was a rolling, cultivated
terrain with a vegetation so luxuriant, in such contrast
to the landscape through which they had passed, that
they might have crossed some border into a semi-tropical
region. Its upkeep must cost a fortune, Venna thought.
Through the grounds ran a well made-up track.

When at last it seemed they must run out of road and
drive into the ocean they came upon Pednolva, a granite-
built house actually constructed into the side of the cliff,
with the front door on the top floor. The three landings
below, Venna marvelled, must stand on rocks not far
above the breaking seas.

'Well, here we are!' Keir braked and switched off the
engine. 'What do you think of it?' He turned and looked
at Venna. He seemed anxious for a favourable reaction.

'It's beautiful. Fascinating. But a little frightening,' she said. 'I've always thought I'd like to live over-looking the sea. But this...' She gestured helplessly.

'You'll soon get used to it. After all, it's your home too, now.'

Venna stared at him.

'I thought this was your mother's home.'

'Yes. But there's plenty of room for all of us.' Humorously, 'You won't be expecting me to throw her out, will you?'

'No, of course not. But I thought we'd...'

'Have a little love-nest of our own? You'll have me to yourself all week, every week, at the flat,' he re-minded her. 'But you don't want that, do you, Venna? As you keep telling me, this isn't a love-match.' He dropped the mocking tone as he went on, 'Let's wake Gemma up, shall we, and take her to meet her grand-mother? I'll carry her.'

Venna received only a brief impression of the entrance hall, its generous, graceful proportions, as she followed in Keir's limping but rapid wake. But as they descended two flights of stairs she realised that the décor of the house was vastly different from that of the London flat.

Soft neutral tones set off antique furnishings and re-strained arrangements of accessories, while retaining simplicity of colour and line.

'I imagine this is more to your taste than the flat,' Keir said. And as she nodded, he said, 'Mine, too. My mother has her own suite of rooms on the bottom floor.' Amusement crept into his voice. 'You may find it a little overwhelming.'

She thought at first he was referring to the encounter with his mother. But as they entered Mrs Trevelyan's rooms she saw what he meant.

It was like moving into a fantasy world. The sur-roundings bewildered the eye. The more she looked, the more she could see—primitive art, chinoiserie, faded dry flowers, religious figures.

Despite the proportions of the rooms, they seemed small and claustrophobic with their rich colours, dense patterns, tactile textures. Oriental rugs in crimsons, reds and purples scattered the floor. Embroidered and patchwork cushions strewed the cane sofa, on which, she saw now, Mrs Trevelyan sat. She and her bizarre surroundings were reflected by two heavy, decorative mirrors.

'You must be Venna.' There was nothing but friend-liness in the older woman's smile. Venna had expected to be scrutinised, perhaps regarded with hostility. 'Welcome to Pednolva. And this...this is Tristram's child.'

As Mrs Trevelyan turned her attention to Gemma, Venna was able to observe the older woman. She was amazingly erect for someone who had to be approaching seventy. She was impressive in a gaudy, flowing caftan similar to that which Venna remembered from Keir's photographs. And she was hung about with various trailing scarves and beads. But Mrs Trevelyan must have lost weight since those snapshots had been taken, Venna thought. She was tall, but very frail-looking.

'Thank you for bringing Tristram's daughter to see me. I understand she's been quite ill. Thank God she survived.' As the older woman turned to speak to her, Venna saw that the grey eyes, so like Keir's were misted with tears. 'Keir said Gemma was like Maria, and she is. But she has a look of Tristram too, don't you think?' She seemed to wait with great eagerness for Venna's reply, and now her eyes were as intent as ever her son's had been. Venna couldn't disappoint her.

'Yes. I think she's like him, too.' At her words, an incomprehensible sound had come from Keir's direction, but when she looked at him he was quite expressionless. She wished she could peel away the layers from those inscrutable eyes to find out what went on in the brain behind them.

'There's a meal ready for you,' Mrs Trevelyan said, 'but perhaps you'd like to see your rooms first and freshen up.'

'Yes, please,' Venna said gratefully. Travelling always made her feel a mess.

'Do you think Gemma would stay with me for a while?' Mrs Trevelyan asked wistfully. 'I'd like to get to know her.'

'She'll stay,' Venna assured her. 'She isn't a bit shy.'

Keir led the way back upstairs.

'My mother has the whole of the ground floor. The drawing-room and dining-room are on the top floor. My rooms are in the middle of the house. It may seem a little strange at first, but you'll get used to it.' He threw open a door and ushered her in. 'Here we are. Don't bother to unpack everything yet, just a dress. We usually change for dinner.'

He shut the door, shrugged off his jacket, then moved across the room, unfastening the buttons of his shirt.

'What are you doing?' Venna demanded.

'I'm going to shower and change for dinner.' Calmly he removed the shirt, revealing a broad chest covered with a fine mat of dark hair that looked sensuously soft.

'Not here! Not in my room!'

'What makes you think it's your exclusive property? This, my dear Venna, is *our* room.' He unfastened the waistband of his trousers and calmly stepped out of them. Dark hairs, not too thick, but definitely sexy, curled on strong calves and thighs.

'I'm not sharing with *you*!' Venna's heart was thudding with panic—and with something else. She was unable to drag her fascinated gaze away from his body.

'Why not?'

'You know why not. I won't... I can't... We had separate rooms at the flat. I want a room of my own here.'

'Impossible!' he drawled. 'What would the servants think?'

'Damn the servants!'

'Oh, by all means!' He was laughing at her again. 'But in actual fact there is no other room available.'

'I don't believe you!' She stalked towards the door and he followed her along the landing. He was apparently quite uninhibited by his practically naked state. She threw open the next door. It was furnished as a study-cum-sitting-room.

'My den,' he told her.

'And this?'

'That's the library. The one you're going to catalogue, remember?'

'I remember. But I didn't know it was going to be your personal library.' And right now even her love of books could not distract her. She moved on. This time it was a bedroom.

'That's my cousin Nick's room. He's home at the moment, so I'm afraid you can't have that. And that's the only spare bedroom.'

'Where's Gemma sleeping?' she demanded, continuing her progress around the landing.

'Here.' This time he opened the door himself.

'Then I'll sleep with her.' But the room was small, and with its built-in furniture only large enough to hold a cot, a chair and a few playthings. 'What about the servants' quarters?'

'They're in a converted outhouse in the grounds, well away from the main building. And before you can suggest you move in there...'

'I wasn't going to.' Even in her desperation, Venna realised the impropriety of thus advertising the mockery of their marriage.

'Oh, good! Then you're becoming reconciled to the idea of sharing with me?' He wasn't even bothering to try to conceal his amusement now, she thought furiously.

'No, I'm not!' she snapped. She stalked back into his room, and with appalled fascination surveyed the large double bed. She couldn't share it with him, she just couldn't. It wouldn't have been so bad if there had been two single beds. 'If you were a gentleman,' she told him, 'you'd offer to sleep on the couch in there.' She nodded towards the door which must adjoin his study.

'True,' he agreed. 'But being a gentleman doesn't always get you what you want in life.'

'If you mean what I think you mean,' she retorted, 'being a louse isn't going to get it for you, either.' She opened her suitcase and dragged out the clothes she needed for the evening, stalked to the ensuite bathroom and locked herself in.

When she emerged a full quarter of an hour later she was fully dressed and made-up. She deliberately hadn't hurried. She would make him wait. Let him see how inconvenient sharing his quarters could be.

But Keir was ready. At the revealing expression on her face he laughed.

'We may not have many spare bedrooms. But we do have a spare bathroom!' He surveyed her appearance. 'As always, you look very lovely.'

She had chosen dramatic black velvet. Black, she knew, made her hair more gloriously colourful. The outfit consisted of a short, frog-fastening jacket and gored skirt, worn with a demure white blouse.

She'd always been aware of his attraction too, no matter what he had worn, whether formal or casual wear, but now, in tailored evening black with a white dress shirt . . .

'What's wrong, Venna?' He was all concern. 'You've gone quite pale.'

'N-nothing. At least . . . that is . . . I think I may have run the shower too hot.'

'Here.' He pulled out a chair. 'Sit down for a moment.' His hand was at her elbow, guiding her, but hastily she drew away.

'No. I'm all right now. We'd better not keep your mother waiting.' And she didn't want to be alone with him right now, not when all her defences were at their lowest ebb.

She hoped the Trevelyans kept late hours, she thought fervently as they ascended the remaining flight of stairs. The later they retired, the better. With any luck, the long drive today would have tired Keir and he wouldn't be inclined for seduction.

In the dining-room, as elsewhere in the house, there was simplicity and good taste. An enormous carved sideboard occupied the full length of one wall. Its triple mirrors reflected glass, decanters, potted ferns and ivies. More ivies stood either end of a graceful white marble fireplace. An oak table with leather-seated chairs stood in the centre of the room.

Mrs Trevelyan was already at the table, together with a good-looking blond young man who stood up as they entered. Keir introduced him briefly as his cousin Nicholas Trevelyan. There was no sign of Gemma. She had been given a light meal and put to bed, Mrs Trevelyan explained. Venna felt a little resentful that she hadn't been consulted. But her first day here was not the time to start making complaints.

The atmosphere over the meal was easy and pleasant. There were no embarrassing references to Tristram Trevelyan. Mrs Trevelyan was charming to Venna, and she began to wonder if Keir had told his mother the exact truth about her, or at least the truth as he knew it. Surely Mrs Trevelyan would not be so friendly towards someone she blamed for her younger son's death?

The evening came to an end all too soon for Venna. Demelza Trevelyan did not keep late hours, and Nicholas, apparently, had work to do.

'And I expect you're tired, aren't you, dear, after your long drive?' Mrs Trevelyan asked.

Venna was shattered, physically and emotionally. But, 'Oh, no!' she said with forced brightness. 'After all, I was only the passenger. It's much worse for the driver.'

'But if you think that means I'm going to be snoring in five minutes,' Keir said, *sotto voce*, as he escorted her back to their room, 'you couldn't be more wrong.'

CHAPTER TEN

'WELL you needn't think you're going to subject me to any more sexual harassment,' Venna hissed back.

'Is that what you call it?' he said with deep interest as he opened Gemma's bedroom door and swiftly checked that the child was all right. 'I call it making love.'

'And I tell you what you want isn't love. It's...'

'Oh, but it is, Venna.' They were in their own room now and he closed the door and leaned on it, arms folded across his broad chest. Almost as if he suspected her of planning to bolt. Then electrified her by adding, 'I think it's time we made our marriage more than one in name only. You see, I happen to love you very much, Mrs Trevelyan.' He said it with a light matter-of-factness.

'I don't believe you.' It was a cruel joke and her voice was flat.

'Believe it, Venna!' he said emphatically.

'No!' she protested. 'How can I? When you're just saying it because you think that's what I want to hear, that it will make me give in and let you...'

'Why should I think that's what you want to hear,' he demanded, moving towards her, 'when you don't want to be loved? That *is* what you told Tris, isn't is?' He watched her carefully, and, unable to endure the penetrating scrutiny, Venna turned away and went over to the dressing-table. She sat down and with an exaggerated show of concentration began to remove her make-up. But her mind wasn't really on what she was doing.

She wondered what Keir was up to now. She would be every kind of a fool to believe he'd fallen in love with her. She remembered something he'd once said to her, about having passed safely through the dangerous years of stupid infatuations, that he didn't believe in love any more than she did. Unaware that she did so, she sighed deeply. Because Venna—the Venna he didn't know—*did* want to be loved.

He came to stand behind her and his strong hands rested heavily on her shoulders, moved caressingly on the delicate bones.

'You didn't answer my question. Did you or did you not tell Tris you didn't want love?'

Now was the moment when she ought to summon up her courage and tell him about Shelagh and his brother. She stared at her reflection in the mirror. Without make-up her face looked stripped and vulnerable, and she felt she needed to be suitably armoured to face Keir's inevitable wrath when he learned the whole truth. She shrugged his hands from her shoulders and stood up.

'I don't want to talk about that right now,' she told him. 'I'm tired.' To her surprise he made no attempt to restrain her as she picked up her toilet things and her nightdress and headed for the bathroom.

'Venna?' And, as she paused to look at him, 'You don't have to undress in there,' he told her, suspiciously straight-faced. And added, 'I shan't be in the least embarrassed.' In spite of the heaviness she felt, a brief spurt of amusement rose to her lips, which she quickly repressed.

'Perhaps not,' she retorted, 'but I would be.'

As she showered and brushed her teeth, Venna reflected that Keir had been in a very strange mood altogether for the last twenty-four hours. The understandable hostility that had never lain far beneath the surface of his manner towards her had been replaced by this quizzical mischievousness to which her own sense of humour longed to respond.

But she couldn't seriously believe that this change had anything to do with her. It was more likely that he was pleased to be home. It was obvious that he was very much attached to Pednolva and to his mother.

Ten minutes later, when she emerged from the bathroom, there was no sign of him, and Venna decided she would go and look in on Gemma one last time before retiring. Belting her négligé about her slim waist, she stepped out on to the landing.

Nicholas Trevelyan was just going towards his room. She gave him a friendly smile and he paused, blocking her way, apparently nothing loath to chat with an attractive woman, even if she was his cousin's wife.

'We didn't get much chance to talk over dinner,' he said. 'Keir and Aunt Demelza monopolised the conversation.' He gave Venna a considering look. 'I must say I was quite staggered to find old Keir had succumbed to the lure of matrimony. In the past he went to all kinds of lengths to avoid it. Tris was the romantic one. The one who wanted to get married. Did you know Tris at all?'

'Of course she did. She knew him very well, didn't you, Venna?'

She spun on her heel. Keir had come up behind them so quietly that for once she hadn't been aware of his presence. He wore only a brief towelling robe that revealed muscular thighs on which damp hairs lay in tight, flat curls. She swallowed and averted her eyes.

'Y-yes, I knew Tris,' she agreed faintly.

'Were you looking for me, my dear?' Keir stared pointedly at her nightdress and the flimsy matching robe. 'I'm sorry to have kept you waiting.' He slid a firm hand around her waist, pressing her to his side. Through her filmy garments his touch seemed to sear her flesh. To Nicholas he said, 'New brides get so impatient.'

Venna thought the young man looked as embarrassed as she felt.

'Actually,' she was stung to retort, 'I didn't want you at all. I was going to look in on Gemma.'

He wasn't a whit abashed.

'Then we'll go together, shall we? If Nicholas will excuse us,' he added pointedly.

'Oh—of course.' Nicholas Trevelyan stepped hastily out of the way.

As they stood at the child's bedside, Keir's hand slid up from Venna's waist to cup her breast, his thumb circling her nipple in an intensely intimate, mesmeric gesture. She was dismayed to feel herself quiver responsively, and he didn't miss her reaction.

'Shall we go to bed now?' he murmured invitingly against her hair.

Gemma was still sleeping soundly, and Venna could find no excuse to linger at her bedside. Reluctantly she allowed him to usher her back to their room. Her brain squirrelled frantically as she wondered how she could avoid what must surely follow.

'Ladies first!' He gestured invitingly to the bed. His sensuous mouth was quirked into an odd little smile.

'Keir, please, I . . .' Her voice trailed away at the implacable expression in his eyes. With trembling fingers she unfastened her négligé and scrambled between the sheets, pulling them up closely around her neck. She swallowed convulsively and closed her eyes as he unbelted his robe. If she were to catch sight of that magnificent muscular body she would be utterly lost.

But she couldn't remain unaware of the fact that he was in the bed beside her and she tried to edge away. But he'd noticed the would-be unobtrusive movement and he merely shifted closer.

'Why all this virginal coyness, Venna?' he asked. She could sense him leaning over her, studying her face.

'After all, it's not as if you haven't seen a man's body before, is it, or made love to him? Is it?' he persisted.

This was the moment to confess, before things got out of hand. She screwed her eyes up even tighter against tears that pricked behind them. He was going to be so angry with her. But before she could think where to begin his mouth took hers in a kiss which demolished any coherent thought she might have had. Unexpectedly, the kiss was sweet and gentle, coaxing her lips apart so that his tongue might explore the soft depths within in imitation of a deeper intimacy.

Venna gave a broken little sigh of pure ecstasy.

The kiss went on and on, drugging her with its sensuality. But apart from that he wasn't touching her, and slowly within her Venna felt frustration began to build. She wanted more than this. Under his mouth she whimpered softly and wriggled her body invitingly closer to his. Blindly her hands sought his shoulders, caressed the smooth, supple skin. As she extended her exploration through the tangle of hairs on his chest, she felt his ribcage lift and fall in a quick, harsh breath.

He was not unmoved by their kisses, so why didn't he touch her? She freed her mouth and let her lips roam the hard angle of his jaw, the strong, tensile cords of his neck. The movements of her mouth became more feverish. She essayed a provocative nibble at his earlobe.

'Keir?' she murmured.

He made no answer, but he recaptured her mouth with tiny, soft kisses, unbearably stirring but unable of themselves to satisfy.

Without her consciously willing it, her hands slid down his ribs towards his hips, shaped the hard, bony structures, ventured further, then stilled for an instant. He was quite naked and, like her, he was unmistakably very aroused. She knew he wanted her and marvelled at the self-control he maintained.

At last, when the agony of wanting became almost too much to bear, he touched her, just the lightest of caresses, his hand sliding across her breasts and down over her stomach in a fugitive torment.

Her body jerked, and desire was so acute within her that it was pain. Then, gently, he mouthed the swollen nubs of her breasts. She grasped his shoulders and tried to pull him down on top of her, but found resistence.

'Please,' she pleaded shamelessly. She wanted to know the weight of his body and the fierce rapture of his possession. Right now, nothing else mattered.

But, incredibly, he was moving away from her. Her eyes flew open and she saw that he was standing by the bed, pulling on his robe.

'So, Venna, you do know what it is to want?' His expression was unfathomable.

'Yes,' she whispered, green eyes anguished. She didn't care right at that moment if he dragged her pride in the dust, so long as he appeased the desire that racked her.

'But you still don't know what it is to love, any more than you did when you gave yourself to my brother? Is that right?'

She was ready then to tell him she loved him, that she didn't care that he didn't love her. But he was removing his pillow from the bed. She sat up.

'W-what are you doing?'

'Earlier you said you wanted me to sleep on the couch in the study. I've decided to do just that.'

'But...' Venna stared at him. She just didn't understand this man. If he'd felt even half the sensations she had known, he wouldn't be able to walk away like this. He wasn't acting like a man suffering from frustration. If anything, she felt that, subtly, he was mocking her again.

As the study door closed behind him she fell back against her pillows with an anguished little moan.

'Oh, God!' she whispered. Desolation and an aching sense of loss swamped her, had to find expression in violent action. She got out of bed and pulled on her négligé. Back and forth across the deep-pile carpet she paced restlessly, trying to come to terms with her unslaked desires.

There was no sound from the study. Keir was probably asleep already, she thought resentfully. He seemed to be able to switch his sexuality on and off like an automaton, using it almost like a... The word 'weapon' sprang unbidden into her mind, bringing her rapid footsteps to a halt. She had been a fool to think his hostility had lessened in any way, that he really desired her for herself. She was still being punished for what Shelagh had done. And here, in the home that had also been Tristram's home, the incentive for Keir to do so must be even greater.

It came to Venna then what she must do. However much personal grief it caused her, even though it would certainly mean the irrevocable loss of Gemma, she must leave Keir. She loved Gemma. But she loved Keir even more. There would be no joy for her in a future spent with him, longing for what she could not have—his love.

Oh, Keir wanted her all right. He might despise her, but he wanted her, and one day he might not be able to hold back. If she let him take her on his terms he would enjoy it. But to her that final commitment would mean far more than sexual satisfaction, and could only pave the way to more unhappiness.

Tomorrow, she vowed, she would tell Keir everything. With that done, she would go back to Southport, square her accounts with Terry and begin a new life somewhere.

She had thought it would be impossible to sleep. But strangely, with her decision taken, she fell into the deep, dreamless slumber of exhaustion.

*   *   *

A trim maid brought her breakfast on a tray.

'Heavens! What time is it?'

'Nine o'clock, Mrs Trevelyan. Mr Trevelyan's had his breakfast. He told me to ask you if you could be ready in an hour. He's taking you out for the day.' The maid's tone conveyed her envious conviction that Keir Trevelyan's wife must be the happiest woman living.

Venna's first impulse was to send a refusal. But then, why not? she thought wearily. It might be easier, away from Pednolva and other people, to untangle the web of lies and deceit in which she had become embroiled, and to tell Keir she wanted a divorce.

They were going to Land's End, Keir told her as she fastened her seat-belt. He seemed to be his normal, matter-of-fact self this morning.

Venna shrugged her acceptance. It didn't matter to her where they went. She'd never been to Land's End, and she supposed it was as good a place as any for a showdown. Besides, she had discovered long ago that fresh air and spectacular scenery were great restorers of perspective. That was why she had always loved the Lake District so much. Against the immensities of nature, personal problems seemed to shrink, to become petty and unimportant.

They stopped for their lunch at what must be surely one of the smallest pubs in existence, one stone-flagged room with high-backed settles, a granite fireplace and bottle-glass windows. Keir ordered traditional Cornish pasties and two shandies.

'You'll be pleased to know your business affairs have been sorted out,' he told her as they ate. 'I had my accountant go over the books. There should be a substantial cheque going into your account in the next week or so.'

The news couldn't have come at a better time. At least now she would have capital to invest in some enterprise, and this time she would choose her business partner more carefully. But her spirits remained at zero.

'Terry's found somebody else, then?'

'Yes. Me.'

'You?' She said it with dismayed disbelief. For one thing, she didn't want to be further beholden to Keir. For another, she couldn't think why a wealthy property magnate like Keir Trevelyan should want half-ownership in a provincial bookshop.

'Me,' he confirmed. 'It seemed the best way to extract you from an awkward situation. And with my finance department keeping a close eye on his income and expenditure, it might even do Little himself a bit of good.' He looked at her expectantly. 'Aren't you pleased?'

'Oh...yes...of course. Thank you. But I...'

'I thought, when you've settled in here a bit, we might look around for another property for you. That's if you still fancy the idea of running a bookshop.' He was making it harder and harder for her to tell him. He would have not only deceit but ingratitude to hold against her. He drained the last of his shandy. 'Shall we make a move, then? I'm looking forward to being at Land's End again. I always find it an exhilarating experience.'

It was that and more. They parked the car and walked out along the rocky spur that ran out into the Atlantic's wild grip. It was a world of rearing cliffs and cascading seas, full of energy and fiery haste. It ought to have dispelled Venna's depression. But it didn't.

Land's End. The name suited the region with its granite bulwarks standing in age-long warfare against the might of the ocean. The dangerous character of the coast was emphasised by the Longships Lighthouse rising from its rocky base, while other rocks nearer the shore ruffled the seas.

Keir's strong arm steadied Venna against the buffeting of the wind. If only she could always have his protection, but against the storms of life.

They stood for a long time looking out to sea, both of them just content to drink in its elemental beauty, each immersed in their own thoughts.

'Look,' Keir pointed with his free hand, 'you can just see the Scilly Isles. Would you like me to take you there some day?' His arm tightened about her. 'After all, we never did have a honeymoon.'

'Mmm,' she said, but it wasn't just his closeness that was causing her abstraction. She had been trying to think of a way to lead up to her subject. She couldn't just come out with a bald statement. As they began to walk back to the car, she asked, 'Keir, what have you told your mother and your cousin about me?'

'The whole truth, and nothing but the truth!' he said with mock gravity, his hand over his heart. Then, 'Why?' he asked with unconcealed interest.

'They seem so friendly,' she puzzled. 'I didn't expect...'

'You didn't expect them to be courteous to my wife?' He was being deliberately obtuse, she thought crossly.

'You know very well I didn't mean that.'

But Keir's thoughts seemed to have gone off at a tangent.

'Did Tris tell you any of the legends associated with Land's End?'

'He...he may have done,' Venna said distractedly. 'But Keir, about your mother...'

'Somewhere out there,' he stopped and looked back towards the mighty bastions of rock, 'is Lyonesse. Some people say it's the original site of Camelot.'

'King Arthur must have been a very busy man,' she retorted, momentarily diverted. 'There are so-called Camelots all over England.'

'Maybe. But I like to think Cornwall has the prior claim. It's fitting, don't you think, that such a beautiful country so full of legend and mystery should be host to one of the greatest legends of them all?'

As he talked, she studied the determined face. Despite the pugnacity of the firm jawline, the strength of rough-hewn features, there was a hint of the other man, the passionate one she knew existed. It was there in the full lips, in the brooding grey eyes. And now, too, she was permitted to see the poetic lilt to his mind. Wonderingly, she realised that he was a man driven by beauty and emotion, not just by the stark motives of sexual appetite. And this was the man who had said he didn't believe in love. This was the man she was planning to leave.

It was the fierceness of the wind coming in off the sea that was making her eyes smart, she told herself as she turned away. It blinded her temporarily to the unevenness of the terrain. She stumbled, feeling her ankle give way, pitching her sideways, so that if it had not been for Keir's swift intervention she would have sprawled full length.

'Throwing yourself at me again! At least this time you didn't get a bump on the head!' he said humorously. His mouth was close by her cheek. His warm breath, clean and wholesome in her nostrils, caused a confused upheaval within her. Alarmed by the sudden tumbling rush of her heart, she tried to twist free, but his strength held her prisoner in his arms. She looked up to protest and caught his grey-eyed gaze intent upon her face.

'Why did you finally agree to marry me, Venna?' he asked suddenly, catching her off guard.

'You...you know why,' she almost whispered, so that he had to bend his head to catch the words. 'For Gemma's sake. And because I made a bargain...'

'I find it very difficult to believe in such perfect altruism,' he said, releasing her and moving towards the car. 'Or that you suddenly discovered a belief in God.' He unlocked the passenger door for her, then took his place behind the wheel. He turned to look at her. 'There must have been something else in it for you,' he pressed.

She swallowed uneasily as she studied his swarthy features and the dark head sprinkled with grey. The hair was thick and vibrant and her need to remind herself of how it felt to the touch was so violent that it almost overcame her. With difficulty, she restrained the urge to caress the springy growth.

'Looking back,' he said as he started the engine, 'I recall that you only agreed after you'd discovered I was a man of some substance.'

'Oh!' As he darted her a sideways glance, her green eyes blazed, as with all the fire of her red-headed temper she shouted at him, 'Don't you dare accuse me of such mercenary motives! I wouldn't care if you didn't have a penny in the world so long as you...' She broke off abruptly from what she had been about to say.

'So long as I what?' The car slowed and his eyes locked with hers with such intensity that she wondered if she had betrayed anything of what she was feeling. She had been going to say—as long as he loved her.

'So long as you didn't separate me from Gemma,' she muttered a substitute as he returned his attention to his driving.

For a mile or so there was silence. But she could almost hear the activity of his brain. He was being more than usually persistent in his questioning today. She ought to have been glad of it. It should have helped her to make her confession. But it didn't.

'And there was nothing more to it than that?' he asked suddenly.

Despite the lapse of time, she didn't have to ask what he meant.

'What else could there be?' she fenced.

'Oh, I don't know.' The car turned in at the gates of Pednolva House. 'Stupid of me, of course, but I thought perhaps you might have developed some sort of fondness for me.' And, while she was still quivering from that remark, 'Seeing Land's End must have brought back a

lot of memories for you, Venna. It was there you first
met Tris, wasn't it?' He braked on the gravel sweep in
front of the house, and turned to look enquiringly at
her.

'Er...yes...I...' Her eyes fell before his appraisal.
Stupid, she told herself. You could have told him it wasn't
you.

'You little liar!' he exclaimed, and her heart lurched,
but it wasn't an angry exclamation. He sounded frankly
amused. He came round to her side of the car and helped
her out. 'You didn't meet anywhere so glamorous.' And
as he steered her firmly through the front door, 'You
met him in a bookshop in Penzance.'

'Oh!' Venna said faintly. 'Of course, I...'

'Don't dig your own grave any deeper, my dear Venna,'
he advised obscurely, urging her towards the stairs down
to their apartment.

She would have stopped in the middle of the flight to
look at him, but he seemed to be in a hurry and, before
she had time to collect her wits, they were in the
bedroom, the door firmly closed behind them—and
locked, she noticed with sudden trepidation, seeing the
key in his hand.

'Wh-why did you do that?' she asked nervously.

He thrust the key in his pocket.

'Because the time has come to put an end to this absurd
masquerade of ours.' He must mean their marriage. Despite the fact that she'd been going to insist on a divorce,
Venna's stomach churned queasily. 'And we're neither
of us leaving this room until we've got it straightened
out.'

'B..but we can't stay in here all that time,' she objected. 'It...it's mid-afternoon. What will your
mother...the servants...?'

'They'll very properly think we've been overcome by
honeymoon madness. No one is going to disturb us under
those circumstances.' He shrugged off his jacket and sat

on the side of the bed. He patted the place beside him invitingly. 'Come here, Venna.'

'I...I'd rather sit over here.' She indicated the dressing-table stool and his brow darkened.

'And *I* said come here.' And as she hesitated his face was suddenly illuminated by a smile. 'Oh, come on, Venna, for heaven's sake. I'm not going to eat you.'

Reluctantly she sat down beside him, and at once his arm snaked about her waist and held firmly. Through the fine material of his shirt his body was warm, infinitely stirring to her senses.

'Now, Venna, we'll have the truth. You never met my brother Tristram in the whole of your life, did you?' he challenged.

Startled she looked up at him, found his face very close to hers, and found she couldn't look away.

'How...how did you know?'

'I didn't—not at first. But there were a few inconsistencies that puzzled me, not least being my own reactions to you. You see,' he said slowly and deliberately, his eyes boring into hers, 'I would never have fallen in love with the type of woman you were supposed to be.'

Venna quivered and tried to look away, but his free hand captured her chin and kept her face turned towards him as he went on.

'Yes, I love you. Oh, I know I said I didn't believe in love. What a crass fool I was! But then, there was some excuse for me.' His voice was suddenly husky. 'I hadn't met *you* before.'

'Keir...' she swallowed. Her green eyes were enormous in a face pale with emotion and her lips quivered invitingly.

'No, let me finish. If I once start kissing you...' He cleared his throat. 'I don't know when I first realised I was in love with you. I do know I fought against it. But the better I got to know you, the more convinced I became that somewhere something was wrong.'

'I hated deceiving you...' Venna began.

'But you were afraid to tell me the truth?' He nodded. 'I can understand that. Because if you'd been the kind of woman I'd expected, I would have moved heaven and earth to get Gemma away from you. But you were so different.' His arm tightened convulsively and she edged closer to him, dared to rest her head on his shoulder. Suddenly she had the feeling that perhaps everything was going to be all right.

'Are you very angry with me?' she asked in a low voice.

'Only for not trusting me—once you knew me better.' He sounded reproachful.

'I'd reached a stage,' she confessed, 'where I *dared* not tell you—not because I didn't trust you, but because... well, for other reasons.'

'What reasons were they, Venna?' he enquired softly. 'Don't you feel able to tell me that now?'

For an instant she hesitated, then courageously she lifted her head and her lovely eyes met his frankly.

'Because I was in love with you,' she told him, 'and I thought, if I told you the truth about me not being Gemma's mother, you'd be furious, that you'd go away and I'd lose not only Gemma, but you.'

He did kiss her then, as though he could not restrain himself any longer. And when he lifted his head again he said shakily, 'I'm ashamed to admit how many times I've been jealous of that dear little girl, knowing that she came first with you.'

'Not any more,' Venna said. 'Oh, it's not that I love her any less.' Her voice quivered with feeling as she went on, 'But I love you in a different way and so very much.'

'And I was even jealous of Tristram,' Keir continued his own personal castigation, 'when I believed you and he had...'

'I'm glad you were jealous,' she said softly. Then, seeing he was about to kiss her again, she put a gentle finger on his mouth. 'But however did you find out the truth?'

Beneath her finger, his mouth widened into a grin.

'Quite by accident, really. Remember the business trip I made, just before we came down to Cornwall? I didn't tell you where I was going, because I was going to Southport. I dealt with your ex-fiancé in person. He didn't like that very much. In fact, he lost his temper. He seemed to gain great satisfaction from telling me about your half-sister, Shelagh, and that you weren't Gemma's real mother. He couldn't know,' again Keir smiled, 'the intense pleasure he was giving me.'

But Venna looked at him doubtfully.

'Keir, you didn't really think I'd married you for your money?'

'I was sure you hadn't,' he reassured her. 'You just weren't that kind of person.'

'And,' she persisted, 'are you sure you were in love with me *before* you found out I wasn't Gemma's mother?'

Keir snorted indignantly and pulled her across his knees.

'Don't dare doubt it. Why do you think I kept on asking you to marry me? I could have looked after the pair of you perfectly well without that. It was a lame excuse. But I didn't know then that you were capable of loving me. I thought I had a long uphill task ahead of me, winning you over.' He was suddenly grave as he said, 'You'll never know the agonies I went through waiting for you to make up your mind.'

'Suppose, in the end, I'd still refused?'

'There wouldn't have been an end,' he told her positively. 'If you remember, I once told you that when I want something I go all out to get it.'

'But why didn't you tell me you knew about Shelagh?' she puzzled. 'As soon as you came back from Southport?'

He grinned wryly.

'I nearly did. I told my mother that same night, on the phone. I was so cock-a-hoop, I told her the whole story from start to finish. But I wanted you to trust me enough to tell me yourself. I kept giving you chances,' he said reproachfully.

'I know. And I'm ashamed of being such a coward. But before we went out I'd made up my mind to tell you the whole truth and ask you for a divorce.'

'What?' His mouth was a grim line.

'Only because I loved you,' she assured him with a quick kiss. 'Because I couldn't bear the thought of living with you and never being able to tell you so, knowing that you didn't love me.'

'And now you know that I do love you?' he asked huskily.

'Oh, Keir,' she felt colour suffuse her face, while warmth invaded the whole of her body as she said, 'now I just want to show you how much I love you. It's been such agony...'

'And for me too, my darling,' he told her fervently. 'If you only knew how difficult it's been to make love to you so far and no further. All along I had this hope that you did love me, that eventually you'd admit it. I knew you were physically attracted to me. I even tormented you sexually in the hope that you'd break.' He grinned ruefully. 'You weren't far wrong, were you, when you called it sexual harassment?'

'I wanted you, too—dreadfully,' she murmured against his mouth. 'In fact,' she admitted with a little throb in her voice, 'if you'd stayed last night you might have found that out a bit sooner. Keir, were you...were you really not punishing me for...for Tristram?'

'Good lord, no!' He said indignantly. 'I don't believe in the "eye for an eye, tooth for a tooth," method. If anyone was being punished,' he added wryly, 'it was me.' Huskily, 'If you knew how difficult it's been to hold back the words, to prevent myself from...' His voice shuddered away on a deep inhalation of breath.

At this, she looked at him longingly, believing him as she saw the lines of strain in his face.

'Then, Keir, couldn't we...?' She stumbled on the words, flushed, became confused as she saw the look in his eyes.

'Yes, my darling, we most certainly could.' His mouth swooped to take hers, and with fingers that shook he began to unfasten the front of her dress.

As they undressed each other she murmured shyly, 'Keir, you do believe me, that it will be the first time for me?'

'I know, my darling,' he said throatily. 'And I feel very honoured, very privileged to be the first one to know your love. But I'd better warn you...' He stopped dramatically.

'Yes?' Alarm made the word catch in her throat.

'I'd better warn you,' he growled, 'I intend to be the last, too.'

Then they were laughing in each other's arms, and laughter eased the moment of tension when, simultaneously strong and gentle, step by step he began to lead her towards the moment she had been waiting for.

Venna felt totally engulfed by his love, by his hard, forceful, exciting body, his beautiful mouth as he declared his need of her. She was sucked up in a storm of emotion such as she had never experienced before, had never expected to experience.

He swept her along with him, his hands lifting her higher and higher, melding her to him. She felt her blood pulsating, throbbing in her veins, throughout her whole body.

He was speaking to her, incomprehensible words and sentences she couldn't hear because she was speaking at the same time, crying out his name. He formed every inch of her body, his hands beguiling, coaxing. At the moment of entering her he kissed her, deeply, intimately, paralleling the movement of his body as she arched upward to meet him. Welded to him, she gave and gloriously took at the same time, held close to him, his for all time.

Spent and dizzy, she lay in his arms, her green eyes sensual with satisfaction.

'Any questions now about whether I love you?' he asked tenderly.

'If that was the answer,' she told him provocatively, 'I shall ask you the same questions every day!'

His response was extremely satisfactory, her reception of him as eager, their coming together as sweet and tender.

'My love,' he asked her after a long, long time had elapsed, 'are we going to stay here all afternoon? Because, much as I'd like to go on making love to you, I find it difficult to think about anything else with you in my arms, and there are plans to be made.'

'Surely we can plan here as well as anywhere else?' she murmured suggestively, her hands caressing the silky hardness of his body.

'It depends what sort of plans you have in mind,' he said absently, as though he found it difficult to concentrate on his thoughts. 'For instance, do you want to go on being career woman? Have we to find that little bookshop for you? Here in Cornwall or...'

'That would mean I'd only see you at weekends,' she objected and, all shyness vanished now, 'I want to be with you always.' After he had kissed her she went on, 'I would like to have my own shop again some day. But that's something I can take up again when the children are older.'

'Children?' He raised his head to look at her and, though she was no longer shy of him, she blushed. 'You did say *children*? Plural? You're planning to have *our* children? As well as Gemma?'

'Don't you want that?' she asked anxiously.

'Want it? Oh, Venna! Words can't express...I can only...' He reached for her again. 'Plans like that we *can* make—here and now.'

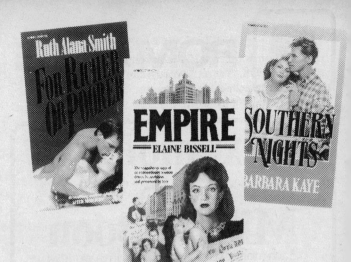

THE POWER, THE PASSION, AND THE PAIN.

EMPIRE – *Elaine Bissell*_____£2.95
Sweeping from the 1920s to modern day, this is the unforgettable saga of Nan Mead. By building an empire of wealth and power she had triumphed in a man's world – yet to win the man she loves she would sacrifice it all.

FOR RICHER OR POORER – *Ruth Alana Smith*_____£2.50
Another compelling, witty novel by the best-selling author of 'After Midnight'. Dazzling socialite, Britt Hutton is drawn to wealthy oil tycoon, Clay Cole. Appearances, though, are not what they seem.

SOUTHERN NIGHTS – *Barbara Kaye*_____£2.25
A tender romance of the Deep South, spanning the wider horizons of New York City. Shannon Parelli tragically loses her husband but when she finds a new lover, the path of true love does not run smooth.

These three new titles will be out in bookshops from December 1988.

W●RLDWIDE

Available from Boots, Martins, John Menzies, WH Smith, Woolworths and other paperback stockists.

 **ROMANCE**

Next month's romances from Mills & Boon

Each month, you can choose from a world of variety in romance with Mills & Boon. These are the new titles to look out for next month.

THE ASKING PRICE Amanda Browning
ONE HOUR OF MAGIC Melinda Cross
STRANDED HEART Vanessa Grant
POOL OF DREAMING Dana James
WILD JUSTICE Joanna Mansell
THE LOVING GIFT Carole Mortimer
CROCODILE CREEK Valerie Parv
A DIFFERENT DREAM Frances Roding
CHASE THE DAWN Kate Walker
TEMPORARY BRIDE Patricia Wilson
ONE RECKLESS MOMENT Jeanne Allan
LORD OF THE LODGE Miriam Macgregor
SOME ENCHANTED EVENING Jenny Arden
LOVE ON A STRING Celia Scott

Buy them from your usual paperback stockist, or write to: Mills & Boon Reader Service, P.O. Box 236, Thornton Rd, Croydon, Surrey CR9 3RU, England. Readers in Southern Africa — write to: Independent Book Services Pty, Postbag X3010, Randburg, 2125, S. Africa.

Mills & Boon
the rose of romance

AND THEN HE KISSED HER...

This is the title of our new venture — an audio tape designed to help you become a successful Mills & Boon author!

In the past, those of you who asked us for advice on how to write for Mills & Boon have been supplied with brief printed guidelines. Our new tape expands on these and, by carefully chosen examples, shows you how to make your story come alive. And we think you'll enjoy listening to it.

You can still get the printed guidelines by writing to our Editorial Department. But, if you would like to have the tape, please send a cheque or postal order for £4.95 (which includes VAT and postage) to:

VAT REG. No. 232 4334 96

AND THEN HE KISSED HER...

To: Mills & Boon Reader Service, FREEPOST, P.O. Box 236, Croydon, Surrey CR9 9EL.

Please send me _____ copies of the audio tape. I enclose a cheque/postal order*, crossed and made payable to Mills & Boon Reader Service, for the sum of £_____. *Please delete whichever is not applicable.

Signature _____

Name (BLOCK LETTERS) _____

Address _____

_____ Post Code _____

YOU MAY BE MAILED WITH OTHER OFFERS AS A RESULT OF THIS APPLICATION   ED1

THREE TOP AUTHORS
THREE TOP STORIES.

TWILIGHT WHISPERS — *Barbara Delinsky* — £3.5
Another superb novel from Barbara Delinsky, author of 'With
Reach' and 'Finger Prints.' This intense saga is the story of th
beautiful Katia Morell, caught up in a whirlwind of power, traged
love and intrigue.

INTO THE LIGHT — *Judith Duncan* — £2.5
The seeds of passion sown long ago have borne bitter fruit fo
Natalie. Can Adam forget his resentment and forgive her for leavin
in this frank and compelling novel of emotional tension and turmoi

AN UNEXPECTED PLEASURE — *Nancy Martin* — £2.2
A top journalist is captured by rebels in Central America and hi
colleague and lover follows him into the same trap. Reality blend
with danger and romance in this dramatic new novel.

Available November 1988

W●RLDWIDE

Available from Boots, Martins, John Menzies, W.H. Smith,
Woolworths and other paperback stockists.

ROMANCE

Next month's romances from Mills & Boon

Each month, you can choose from a world of variety in romance with Mills & Boon. These are the new titles to look out for next month.

FOR KARIN'S SAKE Samantha Day
PILGRIM'S PROGRESS Emma Goldrick
POTENTIAL DANGER Penny Jordan
HURRICANE! Mary Lyons
A STRANGER'S GLANCE Jessica Marchant
PRISONER OF THE MIND Margaret Mayo
A QUESTION OF LOVE Annabel Murray
JUST ANOTHER MARRIED MAN Edwina Shore
ERRANT DAUGHTER Angela Wells
TENDER PERSUASION Sara Wood
FINAL SCORE Jennifer Taylor
THE HUNGRY HEART Margaret Way
SONG OF LOVE Rachel Elliot
ALIEN MOONLIGHT Kate Kingston

Buy them from your usual paperback stockist, or write to: Mills & Boon Reader Service, P.O. Box 236, Thornton Rd, Croydon, Surrey CR9 3RU, England. Readers in Southern Africa — write to: Independent Book Services Pty, Postbag X3010, Randburg, 2125, S. Africa.

Mills & Boon
the rose of romance

ACCEPT 4
MILLS & BOON ROMANCES
ABSOLUTELY FREE

...after all, what better way to continue your enjoyment of the finest stories from the world's foremost romantic authors? This is a very special introductory offer designed for regular readers. Once you've read your four **free** books you can take out a subscription (although there's no obligation at all). Subscribers enjoy many special benefits and all these are described overleaf. ▶▶▶